4/03

D0251407

MY MOTHER'S DAUGHTER

FOUR GREEK GODDESSES SPEAK

Doris Orgel

Illustrated by

Peter Malone

A Neal Porter Book
ROARING BROOK PRESS
Brookfield, Connecticut

Copyright © 2003 by Doris Orgel

Illustrations copyright © 2003 by Peter Malone

A Neal Porter Book

Published by Roaring Brook Press

A Division of The Millbrook Press,

2 Old New Milford Road, Brookfield, Connecticut 06804

Library of Congress Cataloging-in-Publication Data

Orgel, Doris.

My mother's daughter: four goddesses speak / by Doris Orgel ;

illustrated by Peter Malone.–1st ed.   p. cm.

Summary: Four Greek goddesses, Leto and her daughter Artemis, and Demeter and her

daughter Persephone, relate their individual experiences as mothers and daughters.

1. Mythology, Greek–Juvenile fiction.   [1. Mythology, Greek–Fiction.   2. Goddesses–

Fiction.   3. Mothers and daughters–Fiction.]   I. Malone, Peter, 1957-ill.   II.Title.

PZ7.O632 My 2002   [Fic]–dc21   2002023702

ISBN: 0-7613-1693-0 (trade edition)

2   4   6   8   10   9   7   5   3   1

ISBN: 0-7613-2808-4 (library binding)

2   4   6   8   10   9   7   5   3   1

Book design by Jennifer Browne

Printed in the United States of America   First edition

In memory of my mother, Erna Adelberg

❧❧❧❧❧❧

For my daughter, Laura Orgel, and her daughter, Jennifer Kemp

❧❧❧❧

With gratitude to Amy Berkower for her encouragement;
to Neal Porter for his good sense, sharp ear, and humor;
and special thanks to Richard Jackson for his inspiration.

TABLE OF CONTENTS

INTRODUCTION

Leto, Artemis, Persephone, Demeter—their names are musical, mysterious. Who were these mighty goddesses? How did they capture my imagination and compel me to write this book?

We now think of them as mythological figures. Yet it's important to remember that what *we* call mythology was once a religion, as meaningful throughout the ancient Greek and Roman world as our religions are today. It was a formal, ceremonious, and highly personal religion. Its many gods and goddesses (for those included in this book, see pp. 113–120) did not always stay aloof on top of Mount Olympus. They often came to earth and made themselves known—or so their worshipers believed. These worshipers experienced such encounters as sacred and intensely real.

For instance: Imagine a young girl in ancient Greece, released from her domestic chores. She rushes out, she races through woods, exulting in her freedom, and feels as though great Artemis, goddess of the wilderness, is running by her side.

Or a musician, strumming his lyre, feels Apollo's presence and thanks him for putting new tunes into his head.

And poets—Homer, Hesiod, and others—believed that their inspiration came from the Muses Calliope and Clio, goddesses of poetry and history, breathing words into their ears.

Many of the ancient poets' works are lost. But some, notably Homer's *Iliad* and *Odyssey,* and Virgil's *Aenead,* are widely read and loved today. Their stories still enthrall, as do the gods and goddesses depicted in their pages.

These radiant beings dazzled me when I was growing up—especially the goddesses. I loved that they could zoom through space to any place they chose to be, change mortals who displeased them into birds or trees, grow mountain-tall, lift up an island in one hand and hurl it at a foe! It thrilled me that they did such things, and yet, in many ways, they were a lot like us. I thought, *If they're like us, then* we're *like* them*!* This idea delighted me and made me proud to be a girl.

At twelve or thirteen, skimming through Homer, Bulfinch, and Hawthorne's *Twice-Told Tales,* and poring over every word of my favorite book, Sally Benson's *Stories of*

Gods and Heroes, I learned that Zeus and Hera's marriage was rocky (they quarreled, like my parents did!); that Athena was the smartest of all the deities on Mount Olympus; that Aphrodite thought having love affairs was fine, the more the better! I shuddered at Persephone's scary journey to the Underworld, but wondered if she wasn't also a little bit glad to get her bossy mother off her back for just a while. I considered how *I'd* feel if I were parted from *my* mother, whom I adored, yet fought with and resented, whose company I craved, while wishing to be on my own.

That was many years ago. My mother has died, but she is present in my thoughts and in my missing her. And when I remember how we quarreled, I see it from a double vantage point: that of the daughter I still am, and of the mother I've become—and from a third, that of a grandma, too.

These memories and musings led me to Artemis and Leto, Persephone and Demeter, goddesses who clashed with each other, as I did, as mothers and daughters do. I asked myself, what strength of theirs allowed their closeness to prevail over their struggles?

Preparing for this book, I immersed myself in sources (see pp. 121–122). The most useful and inspiring was a collection of richly detailed, but often murky, narratives in verse entitled *The Homeric Hymns.* No one knows who wrote them. "Homeric" only indicates that they stem from the eighth century B.C.E., which is when Homer is thought to have lived.

I read with open eyes *and* ears. I hoped to hear the goddesses' voices. I wanted them to speak to readers of my book directly, to narrate their own "memoirs," as it were.

This is not a traditional approach. But there is no *one* tradition. All retellings, from the most ancient to the newest, belong to the retellers' time and must, to some degree, reflect its styles and sensibilities. That said, is listening for the goddesses' voices so very different from what the ancient poets did when they invoked the Muses to breathe poems into their ears?

As I read on, and thought, and started writing, I began to understand: Daughters, whether goddesses or human, are born out of our mothers' bodies. This is our link to each other. It is as strong as iron. But, unlike iron, it has *give*. It is resilient, like some wondrous fabric yet to be invented. It can expand immeasurably far, and doesn't break. It lets us go our separate ways, and when we're ready, pulls us back. Then, rediscovering each other, like Demeter and Persephone, we are overjoyed.

PART ONE

LETO SPEAKS

Other goddesses outshine me. Mortals seldom mention me. And all they ever say is that I love my children. Yes, I do. My children are my joy. But there's much more to tell.

My mother, Phoebe, is a goddess of the moon. My father, whom I hardly knew, is the Titan Coeus, now imprisoned down in Tartarus. I had an older sister, Asteria—I still do. But few would know her. She is greatly changed.

When we were little, and our father went to war, our mother also left us. "My home is in the sky," she said, "I'll come to visit you from time to time."

We huddled close together, Asteria and I, and quarreled less than other sisters do. In winter we slept in caves. In summer we were happier, bedding down in groves and glens, with nothing to prevent us from gazing at the sky.

We often fancied we could see our mother swinging on the crescent moon, or that it was a cradle and she rocked it to and fro.

"Hush, don't make noise," Asteria said one night, "I think I hear our mother singing . . . "

I kept quiet as a mouse. I listened so hard I almost didn't breathe.

"Leto, can you hear it?"

"I don't know." I couldn't tell if I was really hearing Mother's voice, or merely wishing to. "What song is it?"

"A lullaby," Asteria said. But it didn't lull me. It only made me miss our mother more.

She did come down to see us, but not often, and she never stayed for long.

One night, while Asteria was sleeping and I was feeling lonely, our grandmother, Gaia, rose out of the ground. She is the goddess of the Earth. She sat me in her spacious lap and told me, "Don't be sad."

"Why not? I miss my mother!"

"She is with you, don't you know?"

"Where?"

"Inside the circle."

"What circle?"

"The circle of mothers and daughters."

"I don't see it."

"Even so, it's all around us."

"Here in the grove? And also in the sky?"

"Yes, here, and also there."

"What is it made of?"

"Kinship. Continuity."

I didn't understand those words. I asked, "What does it do?"

"It brings you and your mother close as when you two were one."

"You mean, before she gave me birth?"

"Yes, and as close as your mother, *my* daughter, is to me." Gaia smiled. Unlike the rest of us, she doesn't have eternal youth, but when she smiles, it smoothes her wrinkles, and she looks not quite so old. "Leto, someday *you* may become a mother, just imagine." She gave me kisses. "Now close your eyes and go to sleep." Then she sank back down into the ground.

I stayed awake. I wondered, was it really true about my mother being near? If not, I'd *make* her come—or, at least, I'd try. I stretched my arms as high as I could. I called out, "Moon, shine brighter! Distance, dwindle! Chilly night, grow warm!" And I willed my mother to appear.

Did she? I still could not see her. But when I imagined how I'd feel if she put her arms around me, I folded my own arms and made a cradle. I rocked my someday daughter.

I sang to her and found contentment knowing that when *I* became a mother, I'd be loving, I'd be always near.

Meantime the war in which our father and his brother Titans fought raged on. Their goal was to defend their father, Cronos, against young Zeus, who wanted to dethrone him.

Zeus won. He imprisoned the Titans down in Tartarus, which lies below the Underworld. And he built himself a palace high on Mount Olympus. There, seated on his lofty throne, he now rules the whole world, gods and goddesses, as well as mortals.

One summer night, Asteria and I, now nearly grown, strolled along a pebbled shore. The stars shone brightly down onto the sea. Asteria ran in. She splashed and scooped up water, "Leto, look! I'm catching starlight–" Then she gasped, her breath stuck in her throat, and she had to shield her eyes against the brilliance in the sky as Zeus came striding down.

He called her name.

He is the strongest, handsomest of gods. No goddess, nymph, or human girl had ever told him no.

Asteria turned her back on him.

He held out his arms and pleaded, "Won't you come to me?"

"To be your plaything?" she said boldly.

"No, you'll be my beloved," he replied.

"For how long? A night or two, till the next 'beloved' happens by?" She gazed up at the stars. She was their namesake, after all. Perhaps she heard them coaxing her, "Come join with our reflections . . ."

She plunged into the waves, swam dolphin-fast toward a rock, climbed it, called farewell to me. Then she arched her slender body, dived into the breakers, vanished . . .

How could I have suspected the change she underwent— her body that was made of flesh becoming dark, rich soil in which young trees would root themselves?

I only knew that she was gone. I'd lost her.

Zeus wrapped himself in clouds; he stormed away. And I was all alone.

All through my girlhood years, I had a favorite spot for whiling away summer days: a meadow lush with flowers in the foothills of snowy Mount Parnassus. There I'd lie and listen to the music of the waterfall that hurtles down a cliff and pours itself into a crystal stream.

Sometimes I'd kneel down, dip my head into the froth, and let the music of the waterfall rush into my ears.

One morning, I washed my hair in the stream. My hair is neither raven-black nor golden but plain brown. My eyes are also brown, not violet or cornflower-blue. To be sure, my face and form are pleasing—I am a goddess, after all. But poets had not sung my praises, nor had many lovers wooed me—in fact, not even one.

Therefore, imagine my amazement when Zeus came striding down through clouds—to *me*!

My heart beat wildly. I stood up.

He beckoned. I went to him, and wondered as I entered his embrace: Was I now becoming *more* my true self, or *less*?

More, if gladness was the measure. Less, if size determines self. For suddenly I stood diminished, only inches tall!

Zeus is a master of changes. He can turn into a bull, a swan, or any animal he chooses. He does this to experience other forms of being, so that later, when he changes back, he can value his own godhood all the more. Besides, a change of form is handy when he's having an adventure and hoping that his wife won't find him out.

This time he turned himself—and me—into a pair of speckled quail, as drab and inconspicuous as last year's leaves amidst the grass.

The quail cock bowed. He bobbed his plume. He danced a courtship dance around me, clucking, "Lovely Leto, bob your plume, nod to me, be mine!"

I bobbed, I nodded, I consented.

We joined in love together.

Afterward, while I lay cushioned on his feathered chest, I saw my mother, clearly. She stood on a sliver of the pallid daytime moon, exclaiming, "Let my daughter's son be named for me!"

Son? When I'd known that I would bear a daughter? I even knew her name. The waterfall had sung it to me, many times, and just now, again.

Or was this an illusion? Did Mother know better? Had she gone to Delphi, and had the ancient oracle foretold the truth to her?

The oracle at Delphi is the oldest one on earth. It speaks in muddled utterances, hard to understand. But Gaia, long ago, had taught my mother to unriddle them.

The question that I asked myself was, If the oracle revealed that I would bear a son, why did my heartbeat keep repeating, "Daughter, daughter"?

Then a mighty hope began in me—or was it only wishing? I confided it to Zeus.

It made him wild, exuberant. He sprang to his feet—not a quail's, a god's again. Reckless, he had changed us back without intending to. "Twins! I've never fathered twins before!" he shouted loudly. Everyone on Mount Olympus heard him.

"Faithless husband!" Hera shouted even louder, ripping clouds apart and glaring. "Will you never stop deceiving me?"

"I'll stop, I promise! I'll come back to you!"

Coupling is quickly done. Zeus takes his pleasure and departs.

I lingered in the flowering meadow where I'd come into my bloom, and hugged my hope to me. When the moon turned silver in the darkening sky, I called to Mother, "Tell me, if I am to bear a son, will I bear a daughter, too?"

She did not answer me.

When dawn came I set out for Delphi. It wasn't very far. I knew that I was nearly there when suddenly the earth split open as though it had been slashed in two, and formed a dark, forbidding chasm. Carved into one granite wall was a steep and narrow path. Down that path all questioners must go.

At the bottom of the chasm stands a tripod made of bronze. Coiled around the tripod's feet lay the priestess Pytho, guardian of the oracle.

Her face was leathery and creased. Sparse white hairs grew from her head and chin. Her shoulders were bony, her arms were long and thin. Her flattened breasts hung down below her waist. From there to her tail she was like a serpent, legless, and had to slither, as she could not walk.

"Who disturbs my rest?" she asked in a high, weak voice.

"I, Leto, Phoebe's daughter."

"Ah yes, Zeus's latest conquest." Pytho gave a knowing leer. "You want to learn what is in store? Well, you have come too late. The oracle has already spoken."

"Sacred priestess, tell me, please, what did it prophecy?"

She shrugged. "I'm old. I can't recall."

"Venerable Pytho, let it speak again."

"It wracks me hard. It leaves me drained. But Gaia is the source of Delphi's wisdom, and I am Gaia's servant, and you're her grandchild"—she heaved a sigh—"alas, I can't refuse." She bent down, put her left ear to the floor, and muttered low, guttural sounds.

A booming noise began from deeper down. It rumbled through Pytho, coil for coil, and through the chasm. She quaked and shivered, swung her breasts, shook her head, and flailed her arms about.

Then her wild motions ceased. Her head lolled to the side. Her pupils shrank to dots, her eyes went blank. And through her desiccated lips the oracle spoke:

"A sister lost . . . an island gained . . . an easeful birth . . . another, the brother, in dire travail . . ."

Pytho's head slumped forward.

"Oracle, speak more," I prayed.

But Pytho's lips stayed shut.

I became aware of scratching, grating noises overhead, as though something rough, perhaps metallic, were rubbing against stone.

I looked up—and straight into a pair of poison-yellow eyes. A monstrous head bent toward me.

I shuddered.

"That's just my pet, my nursling," Pytho said, awaking from her trance. "Come, my pretty, don't be shy. Jump down from your ledge."

Down jumped her "pretty nursling"—a giant beast, part serpent like his keeper, but with a dragon's face, and paws, claws, and ears as sharply pointed as the tips of javelins.

He blew a cloud of stench at me.

I squeezed myself against the chasm wall.

"Behave yourself, my darling," Pytho said, "you're frightening our guest."

The "darling" licked her hand, then growled and flicked his tongue at me.

Pytho told me, "You are safe while I have charge of him. You needn't be afraid."

"Yes, be afraid, be terrified," said the serpent-dragon's evil eyes. His girth took up the entire floor.

I had to escape. But how could I cross over to the path?

He bared his fangs, and snarled, as though to dare me, "Just you *try!*"

I stood numb. What could I do? Grow fangs and claws myself? Breathe fire? Unhappily I lacked that power.

Well then, I'd try to work a subtler change: Turn fear into its opposite. Stop quaking. Become brave.

I willed my left foot to stand firm and placed it on the monster's back. Then, quickly, I stretched my right foot forward, whisked it past the monster's jaws, onto the path. Heart in my mouth, I swung the rest of me across and clambered up, with both hands covering my belly, shielding the new life—or new lives?—in me.

It was dusk when I emerged from Pytho's chasm. A storm brewed in the west. Happily I knew of a cave nearby, took refuge there, lay down and slept.

Sometime later in the night the cave filled with a radiance, and—did I dream it?—Hera came to me. She wore a purple mantle. Its folds concealed a burden in her arms. She sat down beside me as though we two were friends, and said, "Leto, listen. I'll tell you a story:

"Long ago, when Zeus and I were newly wed, I assumed —don't laugh!—that he'd forsaken all his other loves and, as my husband, would be true to me.

"I clung to this belief for far too long.

"Then, one day, Athena, the young warrior goddess, burst fully armed from Zeus's head. And he boasted, 'She's my daughter, mine alone! I, a male, have brought her forth, all on my own. Athena has no mother.'

"Of course it wasn't true. All beings, mortal and immortal, have mothers. Athena's mother is the Titan goddess Metis. She gave birth to the new goddess but kept her long inside herself. How she devised the second 'birth' from Zeus's forehead is a story only she could tell.

"I had to face the hurtful truth: *My* husband made love with Metis, and no doubt with many others—and still does," she added, giving me a scathing look. "First I was heartsick, then furious and jealous—what wife would not have been?

"'I'll show him,' I decided. 'I'll take revenge!' And out of rage I did the thing that he could not: I bore a child all on my own—"

Now Hera took her mantle off, and I could see what she was holding: the scaly, spiky, fire-breathing monster—Pytho's horrid pet, but smaller—a tiny baby dragon now!

Hera put him to her breast. He suckled greedily.

"I called him Typhaon, a name for winds and smoke and hurricanes. It's fitting, don't you think? I brought him to a caretaker as hideous as he: the serpent-priestess of the oracle at Delphi. I told him when I left, 'There'll come a time when you shall be my vengeance once again—'" She tore her nipple from her offspring's mouth and shouted, "Now that time has come!"

She set him at my feet, commanding, "Follow close upon these heels, my Typhaon! Pursue this goddess, object of my husband's love and of my hatred, without cease!"

Typhaon swelled to monster size.

"Morpheus, god of dreaming, let me be awake!" I cried, and ran out of the cave.

"You *are* awake," said Hera, coming after me, with Typhaon close behind. "And I will punish you. Not for loving Zeus, a fault of which I'm guilty, too."

"Then why?"

"Because your destiny is to outdo me."

"How?"

"By giving birth to splendid children, mightier and more admired than any children Zeus begot, or will beget, on me. No power on earth or on Olympus can prevent it. But, Leto, you will suffer, and Typhaon shall see to it.

"Monster son of mine, torment her. Hound her footsteps night and day. Never let her from your sight. And, Leto, fare you ill."

Then she rose up to the lofty peak of Mount Parnassus and made her proclamation:

"Hear my warning, hills and valleys, mountain ridges, glades and glens, towns and cities, fields and forests, all places that are rooted to the earth: When Leto nears, turn her away. Don't let her stay, or I will curse you with my wrath!"

Typhaon, breathing noxious flames and threatening to sink his claws into my flesh, drove me ever on, almost to the far ends of the earth.

And every place rejected me.

I fled through every kind of weather: fair and foul, ice and snow, even foul and fair at once, when sunshine broke through pelting rain, when rainbows should have curved across the sky. But, strangely, there were none. And during all those months, in all the lands through which I ran, there were no wars, not even little skirmishes. Is that not curious? Do you wonder why?

I will tell you:

Hera had positioned lookouts on two mountaintops. Their task was to make doubly sure that no place on earth allowed me rest.

One was the goddess Iris. She sat atop Mount Mimas, reminding all the islands not to welcome me. That kept her far too busy to carry out her other duty, putting rainbows in the sky.

✿

The other lookout was Ares, Hera's son. He sat on top of high Mount Haemus, warning all lands on all continents against me. This took his full attention. And since he is the god of war, and fighting can't take place without him, for the first and only time in humans' history, the whole world was at peace.

We goddesses feel hunger pangs when we're deprived of our food, ambrosia. "Have pity, throw me down a bite or two," I'd beg the doves who fly it to Mount Olympus every morning. But Typhaon would lash out with his forepaws, fuming, roaring, and frighten the doves away.

We goddesses get thirsty, too, especially in summertime, when my ordeal began. On Olympus we drink nectar, indescribably delicious. On Earth we must resort to water. But every time I saw a river, or a lake, or stream ahead, Typhaon would make it foul by belching poison vapors over it.

We sweat, and tire, just like mortals. Yet the wetter my brow, and the shorter my breath, the less I despaired, the more hopeful I grew. For summer had turned into autumn; autumn, into winter; and even winter has to yield to the change of seasons.

Trees were coming into bloom. Tender grass caressed my feet. The winds of spring were blowing. And all the while my belly grew. I had no notion where I would give birth, but this much I knew: It had to be soon. No power in the world, not even Hera's fury, could prevent it.

As spring advanced, I lumbered through the land called Attica. When I reached its southern shore, a wind god swept me up and blew me to a rocky island named Ortygia. Typhaon followed, swimming in the sea.

Ortygia means "quail." I took that for a happy omen. But when, like every other place I'd come to, Ortygia refused me, I threw my arms into the air, and cried, "Oh Zeus, what you engendered in me struggles to be born! Where shall I lie down?"

No answer came. Again the wind god swept me up and carried me over a stretch of sea. Typhaon came swimming after me. But the waves grew mountain-tall and caused the beast to jounce and bounce as if he were the merest bit of cork. One wave put out the fire shooting from his nostrils. Another threw him on his back. He grappled like a beetle, flailing to turn right-side-up. Still other waves washed over him. When he managed to resurface, he struggled hard for every gasp and rasp for breath.

He had tormented me so long, and now it was his turn to suffer. There was justice in it. Still, I am not made of stone. It troubled me. "Typhaon, turn back!" I called.

He did turn back; it was either that or drown.

But what had caused the waves to swell so mightily?

A landmass—one that *moved*! An island, floating free! The only island in the world that was not anchored to, nor rooted in, the earthen bottom of the sea! It came cutting through the water faster than a ship manned by a hundred galley slaves, nearer, nearer, I could see its trees, its shore . . .

"An island gained . . ." Who'd said those words to me?

The wind god set me down between a palm and an olive tree.

There was a comfort and a sweetness in the air such as I had never felt in all the time I'd been alone. The island seemed deserted, had no dwellings on it. Yet I felt that I'd come home.

"A sister lost . . . an island gained," the oracle had said. And now my heart said, *She is found!*

I looked up, and saw that Iris had resumed her work: a vaulting rainbow spanned the sky.

"Unanchored island, hear me," Hera's queenly voice called down. "You who were Asteria shall be known as Delos from now on. You upheld my honor by saying no to mighty Zeus. As thanks I now relent and grant you leave to give your sister refuge. Leto, rest. My rage is nearly spent."

I sank onto a grassy knoll and leaned my back against the palm tree's sturdy trunk. My time had come. I did not moan. I felt no pain. A pure, wild name resounded in my mind. It was the name the waterfall had sung. And then my daughter sprang from me.

ARTEMIS SPEAKS

"My daughter, Artemis, is born!" My mother Leto's happy cry resounded through the wilderness. At last it had a goddess of its own!

I am like a hailstorm, suddenly ferocious; soon after, I'm serene and calm, as when the storm abates.

I sport with my nymphs, join in their shouts and laughter. But when I roam through woods alone, or drive my silver chariot through the sky, I am my own best company, fulfilled by solitude.

I go where I choose. I do as I please, obeying no one's wishes but my own.

If, in the frenzy of the chase, I've shot a doe that leaves a helpless fawn behind, I'll keep it safe and care for it. But I won't love hunting any less. To hunt is to kill, and hunting is my joy. Arrows whirring, keen hounds baying—these sounds thrill me. So does every newborn creature's first, fierce cry.

I nourish. I cherish. I rescue. I punish. I guard my honor. I take what is my due.

In the foothills of Parnassus is a meadow where my mother dreamed her girlhood days away. I go there often in my mind. I almost feel the prickly grass, I almost smell the flower scents, I hear the roaring waterfall . . . But when I imagine the moment Zeus appeared, I shudder. For it was then that Leto gave—and lost—herself to love.

I honor it, for in that moment I began.

But when I think of Leto left alone, and of the torments she endured, oh, then I howl and beat my fists against my breast, and swear: *I'll* never lose myself to love and pay its heavy price.

Mother, whom I cherish, I'll be your defender. I'll shoot a dozen arrows straight into the heart of anyone who does you harm. But follow in your footsteps? No! I'll keep myself unto myself, and not succumb to any god or man.

Hera took revenge on her. Typhaon pursued her. On and on she ran. At last, on Delos, she lay down, and did not labor. My birth caused her no pain.

She lifted me up and put me to her breast.

All the time she'd fled from Typhaon, she'd had neither

food nor drink. And yet her milk flowed sweet and rich with nectar, which is the source of immortality.

I sucked my fill, then scrambled to my feet.

I took one wobbly step and fell. Scrambling up a second time, I saw a low-slung creature with large ears—a hare—come rushing toward me and streak past. It put a notion—speed!—into my mind.

"Legs, learn what that large-eared creature knows," I commanded. They obeyed. Soon I was running, running fast!—as I was meant to do.

I ran through fields ablaze with crimson flowers, to an expanse of shade. This was the forest. It held out its branches, inviting me: "Come in!"

Its hues of green, its leafy, earthy, pine-smells, its buzzing, gnawing, warbling noises woke my senses, stirring up such joy in me! I leaped about. I whirled around to music that the wind sang in the trees.

Then the wind began to moan, recalling me to Mother.

She had a second child in her. It struggled to be born. She labored hard—she begged Eleithia, the childbirth goddess, "Come!"

We waited.

"It's no use," my mother moaned. "Eleithia is Hera's

daughter. Hera's still my enemy; she won't let her come. Oh, who will ease my pains?"

"*I* will," I said, and hoped that I'd know how.

I fanned her with palm fronds. I cooled her forehead with water from a nearby spring.

At night I covered her with leaves and moss; then I curled up beside her.

One night her pains subsided. "Look up," she said. "What do you see?"

"A sliver of moon, a goddess curved inside it. Who is she?"

"My mother, Phoebe," Mother said. "Listen, I'll sing you a song that Grandmother Gaia sang to me: 'Mother and daughter, daughter and mother/ in a circle/ joined in perpetuity–'"

"Is 'perpetuity' forever?"

"Yes."

"What if the daughter won't become a mother? Will the circle break?"

"No."

"Why not?"

"Because it's strong. It's made of closeness."

"But can a mother and a daughter still be close when they're apart?"

She smiled and said, "Of course." Then we both fell sound asleep.

Next morning her labor pains returned and continued for eight days and nine nights.

On the ninth morning, she was gone from our bed.

I found her crouched beside the palm where she had given birth to me. She clutched its trunk. "Eleithia, help me now!" she prayed, in vain.

"*I'm* here, I'll help!" I still did not know how. But I took it for a lucky sign that *my* birth had been easy. "Eleithia," I prayed, "if you won't come, at least lend me your skill."

Eleithia heard me. She put courage in my hands. I reached into my mother's womb. I touched a shape, all slick and round. I grasped it tight; I felt it thrusting forward.

"Pull, Artemis!" my mother cried.

I did, with all my might. And so, when I was only nine days old, I helped bring forth a god—my twin!

My hands have never lost their skill.

I'm famous as a hunter and a shooter. I'm feared as an avenger when my anger is aroused. But this is also true of me: I go to mothers, animal and human, and I ease their labor pains. I help bring forth their young. I do it for my mother's sake, to ease her grief that I will bear no children of my own.

Mother named my twin Apollo—Phoebus Apollo, in honor of her mother, Phoebe, who had wished it so.

Phoebe came to us that night. She kissed her namesake on the forehead. "You shall be the god of prophecy, and master of the oracle at Delphi."

"In place of Pytho?" Mother asked. "Will she give up her guardianship?"

"She'll have to. Apollo will see to it, won't you, my new little shining god?" Phoebe tickled him under his chin. He gurgled gleefully.

Then she caught a moonbeam, waved, and rode into the sky.

Humans live a short time but stay infants very long. With us, it's just the opposite: We live forever, but our infancy is brief. Some of us have none at all. Aphrodite rose from the sea full grown. Athena came bursting out of Zeus's head, a hearty, sturdy warrior. And I, as you have heard, was deft and capable from very early on.

Apollo grew quickly, too. In his first two weeks, he learned to play the zither and the flute. At one month,

he made himself a slingshot and practiced flinging pebbles
from it. Soon he got so good at it, he seldom missed
his mark.

One time he shot a beetle off a leaf.

"Well done, my boy!" Zeus shouted down. And suddenly the sky grew dark. Huge wings blocked out the sun.
Zeus's eagle plunged to earth, snatched Apollo in his talons,
and flew him to Olympus.

The moment he returned to us, he started boasting:
"Zeus sat me next to him, he's very proud of me. He made
me leader of the Muses. That means I'm god of all the arts.
And look, he gave me presents: This splendid bow of sup-
plest wood, see how it bends and gleams! Also this quiver,
always full of arrows. I'll be the greatest archer in the world!"

Imagine how this made me feel.

Apollo nailed a target to a tree. I was patient, stood and
watched. Not till he'd shot a hundred arrows did I ask,
"Now may I have a turn?"

He said no.

Well, naturally, whenever he went off to visit his new
followers, the Muses, or to spend time with fellow gods,
I'd borrow the bow, unstring it, restring it, notch arrows
to it, and pull it taut, all that. And one day—whoosh!—

an arrow stuck, dead center, in the target on the tree.

"Father, Zeus, did you see *that*?" I shouted, loud, and scanned the sky for dark, wide wings. But Zeus's eagle did not come for me.

Early one morning, Apollo, his bow well-oiled, his quiver on his back, his eyes aglow with lust for adventure, set out, but would not say where to.

He came back blood-bespattered and triumphant. "Delphi is mine! And Pytho's dead! I lured her from her chasm. She crept forth humbly, head held low—she even called me 'Master.' Then suddenly her tail thrashed out and coiled itself around my throat, so tight, I almost couldn't breathe. I flung her off. I stepped into the air—Zeus taught me how! I shot off arrow upon arrow. I pierced her through and through! Mother, aren't you proud of me? Why do you look dismayed?"

"Pytho was Gaia's servant. Gaia will be angry. You must ask her pardon," Mother said.

"I won't! I've come into my power. I'm rightful god of Delphi now, and of its oracle, and god of much more. Let Gaia try to hurt me, I don't care! She won't succeed. Watch this!" Apollo moved his finger across an open wound below his shoulder—and it closed up and was healed. "You see? I'm god of healing, too!"

And what am I *the goddess of?* I wondered to myself.

Leto looked into my eyes, and said (can every mother overhear her daughter's inmost thoughts?), "Artemis, be patient. You'll come into your power soon."

"Yes, you will, this very day," Apollo said.

His prophecy came true. The clouds above us broke apart. Hermes, the god with quicksilver eyes, flew down on winged sandals, scooped me up, and soared away with me.

"Don't be afraid," he said.

"Afraid?" I tried to say, "Not I," but gasped for breath. The air was thin, the ground was crazily atilt, the clouds— and my senses—were spinning round and round.

"We all get dizzy on our first trip through the sky," Hermes said. "Look, we're nearly there."

Faster than thoughts fly through the mind, we reached the mountaintop that storms don't lash and mortals can't attain: Olympus!

Before us stood a palace a thousand times more splendid than the palace of the richest king on earth.

The portals swung open. We proceeded through a hall with alabaster walls and a vaulted, star-emblazoned ceiling, toward Zeus's golden throne.

"Here's Artemis, your brave new daughter." Hermes

set me down on Zeus's knee, and left us two alone.

Zeus is the king of everyone, ruler of the world. Even so, I had to laugh because his beard was tickling my cheek.

"You laugh in *my* presence? Hermes was right, you're brave," Zeus said. "And just how new are you?"

"Three or so years old," I said. (We goddesses don't keep strict count.) "But in many ways I'm nearly grown."

"So I see. Now, brave and nearly grown new daughter, tell me your wishes."

"Well, to start, I want the moon—"

"Not a small request. And what will you do with it?"

"I want to be a moon goddess, like my grandmother, and visit her up there. I'd also like a silver chariot, and four white stags to pull it through the air."

"I see. What else?"

"All forests, all mountains, all wildernesses on the earth. Dominion over wild animals, and to be a hunter beyond compare."

"With what weapons?"

"An excellent bow. Sharp arrows. A quiver always full."

"And will you hunt alone? Or do you want companions?"

"Companions, please: twenty wood nymphs, ten water nymphs, all young like me. And eager hunting hounds."

"That's quite a lot of wishes. How many shall I grant? I know: Perhaps I'll grant them all. Wouldn't that be generous of me?"

"Yes, but I have one more wish."

"Let me guess: to marry a handsome god someday?"

"*No.* To stay a maiden."

"For how long?"

"Forever."

"Are you certain?"

"Yes, because I never want to suffer as my mother did."

His sky-blue eyes went dark. He didn't like to be reminded, and slid me off his knee.

The scent of apple blossoms drifted in. A goddess, very beautiful, appeared. "Aphrodite!" Zeus cried, and ran to her.

She swept past him, toward me. Her violet eyes flashed mockingly. "You wish to stay a *maiden*? For all eternity?"

"She's just a child," Zeus said on my behalf. "She cannot yet imagine the sweetness of your gifts."

"Being free, unto myself, is all the sweetness I will need," I said, speaking on my own behalf.

Aphrodite laughed her famous laughter. Poets call it "golden," but I thought it cold and hard. She snapped her fingers, and six white doves came flying in.

"Don't leave," Zeus begged. But the doves took the

folds of her gown in their beaks and wafted her away.

Zeus sat me back on his knee. He frowned. "You spoke foolishly to her. She is a mighty goddess. You'll regret it. And someday you'll take back that wish of yours." He shook his head, as though to shake my wish away. "Now, as for your other wishes: the moon, a stag-drawn chariot, mountains, woods and wildernesses, dominion over forest animals, and to be a hunter beyond compare . . ." He snapped his fingers. "Done."

"What about my bow and arrows, quiver, nymphs, and hunting hounds?"

"Aren't you eager for adventure? Don't you want to get those for yourself?"

"Yes, and I will."

"Then listen carefully." Zeus told me where to go, and whose help to enlist.

Hermes was waiting by the gates, "Where shall I take you next?" he asked.

"To an island with a fiery mountain on it in the western sea. But I want to go there by myself."

"Very well, I'll teach you how: Climb onto that cloud to your left. Point your toes to the west."

"Like this?"

"Just so. Spread your arms. Say the island's name."

"Lipara!" And faster than an eagle's wings, my own strong will propelled me there.

I landed on a mountain by a crater in which fire smoldered.

Three Cyclopes clumped toward me. They were ten times taller than the tallest man. From each one's forehead glared a single eye.

"What manner of laughably small creature are you?" roared the fattest Cyclops. He pointed his finger, thick as a tree trunk, at me. "Why do you disturb us? We are busy, down at our forge. We have to make a feeding trough for Poseidon's horses."

"Poseidon's horses can wait," I said. "First, make me a supple bow; also, fifty arrows sharper than porcupines' quills; a quiver that can always fill itself with fifty arrows more, and, please, emblazon woodland scenes upon it."

"Is that all? Are you sure?" the ugliest Cyclops asked, and they all laughed at me.

"Who brought you here?" asked the fattest.

"No one. I came by myself."

"From where?" the ugliest asked.

"Mount Olympus."

"Ah, so you're a goddess," said the hairiest, and bowed

to me as though in awe. But then he snatched me up. "Give us a little kiss!" He laughed. He puckered his bulbous lips— and let out a terrible yowl. For I'd grabbed a handful of the thick hairs on his furry chest and pulled and pulled, and didn't stop till he loosened his grip on me.

"I won't give kisses." I jumped to the ground.

He rubbed the stinging, hairless spot and groaned.

I asked, "Now will you make what I need?"

They still would not.

"But you're such famous silversmiths," I said, trying flattery.

"We are," they said, but did not budge.

"Cyclopes, don't forget, Zeus is my father. Therefore, please do what I say, or else—"

"Or else what?" they asked with big, wide grins.

"He'll fling you down to Tartarus, or someplace worse!"

That sent them, fast as they could clump, back to their forge inside the crater.

I sat on the rim, with my feet dangling down, and watched. They blew into their bellows and made the fire hotter. They plunged their hands into the flames, pulled massive chunks of silver out, hammered them flat and round. Admiring how skillfully they worked, I almost forgot how rude they'd been.

Soon they came out and handed me my bow and my quiver, which was full and had woodland scenes emblazoned on it.

I tested it by taking all the arrows out. At once it filled itself with fifty arrows more.

"Are you satisfied?" the fattest Cyclops asked.

"Yes, very."

"Even though the bow stands twice as tall as you? How will you shoot with it?"

"Unerringly. I'll soon be taller. As thanks I'll bring you the first ferocious beast I shoot. Until then, Cyclopes, farewell."

From Lipara I traveled to Crete. I chose twenty wood nymphs from among the many who lived on Mount Leucus, and asked, "Will you come away with me and be my helpers and my friends?"

"Yes!" they answered.

They were all nine years old. True, I was only three or so, but just as tall and strong as they, for nymphs are lesser deities, and don't grow up as fast as I had done.

I also chose ten water nymphs from a nearby river.

They formed a circle, joining hands. I stood in the middle and described how we would hunt and sport together, never tiring of the woodlands' pleasures or one another's company. I told them that I'd pledged to stay a maiden, and asked if they would, too.

They all pledged they would.

I warned them that I would punish whomever broke her word.

Just then I heard a noise, a grunting, in the underbrush. Before I could reach for an arrow, the nymph Callisto had whisked one from my quiver and handed it to me. I notched it to my bowstring, pulled, let go. The arrow pierced the air with a thrilling whir and brought down my first prey.

"Halloo, halloo!" I shouted loudly, as seasoned hunters do. Not having any hounds as yet, I ran and fetched the prey myself—a long-snouted, black-bristled, meaty young boar.

My nymphs looked on and wished that they had weapons, too. Right then I thought of a way I could get bows, arrows, and quivers for them all.

"Back so soon?" the Cyclopes exclaimed when we returned to Lipara.

"Yes, to keep my promise. Cyclopes, look! I bring you this first beast I shot: a tasty, fresh-killed boar."

They snatched it from me. They drove a sharpened spit through its carcass, roasted it over the fire, and ate it

44

up–hide, hooves, and bristles–noisily smacking their lips.

"That was a succulent morsel," said the one whose chest hairs I'd pulled out.

"But scanty," the ugliest said.

"It only whetted my appetite," the fattest one said.

"Bring us more!"

"We could. We might. My nymphs all want to be hunters, too–"

"More boar!" the fattest Cyclops shouted.

"Hear, hear!" the others joined in. "We want rabbits, pigeons, pheasants, hares, wild bulls, and deer, and ducks!"

"My nymphs would gladly shoot all of those and bring you their first prey," I said. "Alas, they can't."

"Why not?"

"Because they have no bows, no arrows."

"We'll make them some, and quivers, too," the Cyclopes said, and heated up their fire.

"When you have your weapons, join me in Arcadia," I told the nymphs. Then I hurried to that pleasant land, to visit Pan, the god of goats and breeder of good hounds.

Pan was busy cutting up a lynx. Hounds of every size and color crowded around him, yapping and yelping for their share.

I helped him feed the hungry horde. He asked, "What may I do for you?"

"I'm a hunter, you see. My nymph-companions will be hunters, too. Would you kindly give us hunting hounds?"

He grinned and tweaked my cheek. "Why not? Take your pick."

I chose one hound with black spots, one with brown, and the two with the longest ears. Those were very brave, Pan said. They'd caught a lion by his mane and dragged him to their lair. I also chose seven Spartan hounds that looked to be the fastest.

"Little hunter, you chose well." Pan winked a yellow eye at me. "Come back when you are older. And bring your nymphs. I'm very fond of nymphs."

"But we've all pledged to stay maidens," I told him.

"What a pity." Pan shook his head and laughed regretfully.

We hunted in Arcadia, my nymphs and I; in Thrace, in Thessaly, and all the lands with wooded groves and mountains. Year in, year out, we sharpened our skills.

They were devoted helpers. They kept my bow well-oiled and ready. They sewed me buskins out of hides. They washed my tunics in lakes and rivers. They fed and cared for our hounds whenever I was away.

But my finest tunic with the crimson border, and my favorite hound, named Lelaps, I entrusted only to Callisto's care. Ever since she'd handed me the arrow with which I'd slain my first prey, she'd been my best companion.

It was Callisto who, one summer day, caught sight of the intruder.

We were bathing, she and I, in a crystal pool among the rocks high on a mountain. I lay afloat, eyes shut. Suddenly Callisto started splashing, churning the water, making it froth.

"Stop!" I cried. "What are you doing?"

"Covering your nakedness. Shielding you–"

"From what? From whom?"

"Look, over there, behind that boulder!"

"I see nothing."

"There! Look now!"

Yes, now I saw a face behind a thicket. And I heard hounds barking. "It's a hunter," I said. "Be calm, Callisto. Let him feast his eyes."

"But he will boast to everyone, 'I saw great Artemis naked!'"

"No, he won't, you needn't fear." I lay back and

floated at my ease, affording the hunter full view.

He tiptoed nearer.

I filled my hands with water and breathed my will on it. He tiptoed even nearer. I dashed the water in his face.

He blinked. His hands went to his forehead—from which antlers sprouted. He opened his mouth, but no words came out, only inhuman groans. His jaw grew long. His ears stood up. His arms became legs. His hands and feet became hoofs. His clothes and skin grew hairs, became a hide. And now *I* was the watcher, looking on as this intruder, Actaeon by name, became a stag.

That was how I punished him for prying.

What then took place was *not* my doing. His hounds caught his scent. They came running, the whole pack. "Stop, I am your master," he tried to shout, but could not.

They nipped at his legs, his flanks. They leaped on his back. They brought him to the ground. They sank their teeth into his flesh, and mangled him to death.

You think that was a cruel punishment? Wait, I'll tell you about Niobe.

She was Queen of Thebes, and proud—too proud—of her twelve fine-looking daughters and sons. One day—it was a feast day in our mother's honor—this queen and her brood were sporting, playing games, and singing songs on a sunny slope of Mount Cithaeron.

Apollo and I chanced to be hunting on that mountain, and overheard the woman boast: "My children are remarkable, so handsome and so fair! Why honor Leto on this day, when *I* have twelve, and she has only two?"

As though with a single will, Apollo and I took aim. We shot five arrows each. His arrows felled five sons, and mine, five daughters.

This was just and right. For now the boastful queen was left with two: no more, no fewer, children than our mother has, with whom she, a mortal, never should have dared compare herself.

Niobe wept torrents, and prayed, "Zeus, turn me to stone, or let me weep forever!"

Zeus granted both of her prayers. If you should climb up Mount Cithaeron, you'll come to a stone shaped like a woman, and from its eyes pour tears in endless streams.

This next story makes me wish that goddesses could weep.

It happened on a sultry day. I and my nymphs—all but my dear Callisto—were bathing in our crystal woodland pool.

She sat on a rock, fully clothed.

I teased, "Are you afraid another hunter will come and spy on us?"

She blushed.

"Undress, jump in, come swim with us."

She'd always done whatever I had asked. But this time she refused.

"Callisto, what's the matter? Are you ill?"

She didn't answer me.

Nephele, who envied her, spoke up. "Callisto is not *ill*." She pulled Callisto's tunic up over Callisto's belly, which, I now saw, was swollen.

"You broke your pledge!" I screamed. "You gave your maidenhood away!"

"Not '*gave*.' A god—I'll not say who—took it by force."

"What god? I order you to say his name."

"It was your father, Zeus."

"You're lying! False friend, out of my sight!"

I turned away. When I turned back Callisto was gone.

In her place stood a bear. It looked at me with deep, dark brown eyes, gave a sadder growl than any bear had ever growled, and trudged away.

I was appalled. Could what Callisto said be true? And who had worked the transformation? Zeus, to hide his latest conquest? Or Hera, jealous once again? I never learned the answer. Nor could I have changed the bear back into my dear, good friend. What one immortal brings about, another can't undo.

Sometime later, roving through the woods, I shot a random arrow off into the blue, or so I thought. It struck a bear. Only when the beast lay dying did I see that she was ripe for giving birth.

I knelt down and delivered her, not of a bear cub—but a baby boy. His hair was raven-black, just like Callisto's. But Callisto's eyes had been dark brown, and his were blue as the sky.

I washed him clean and started rocking him. But Zeus's eagle came flying down, snatched the baby from my arms, and flew away with him.

Which part of this story is the saddest? That it was I who shot the bear? Or that my father, raping my best friend, had done us both a cruel wrong?

Sometimes, heaping blame on Zeus, I choke on my own bitterness. But when I think how sad it is that he, the greatest god, is defenseless in the hands of Aphrodite and must obey her every whim, then my anger softens, and I almost pity him.

One time, missing my lost friend, I harnessed my stags to my chariot and drove and drove the whole night through. I hoped to reach the constellation that Zeus had named "The Bear" and put into the sky. But it was higher than the moon and much too far away.

Years later, while strolling through the woods, I came upon a curly-headed little girl. In time I grew as fond of her as if she'd been my daughter.

Her father was King Iasus of Arcadia. "I wanted a *son!*" he'd complained at her birth and ordered a servant to leave her on a mountainside, exposed to winds and snow.

Luckily a mother bear had brought the baby to her den and suckled her along with her own young.

She was some two years old when I first saw her, romping with her bear cub foster-brothers near the den. They pummeled her; she cheerfully pummeled them back.

She smiled when I approached, held out her chubby hands to me. I picked her up and saw a heart-shaped birthmark on her wrist.

I visited her often. I taught her to speak, to stand upright, to walk, and to run, which she did very well. Soon Atalanta (that's the name I gave her) could run faster on two feet than hares and deer on four.

When she got a little older, I taught her to hunt and shoot. She had a flair for both.

One time she asked me, "What do other girls, not bear-girls, do?"

"What their fathers tell them to: spin and weave, cook

and clean, help take care of younger children in the household."

"What do they do when they grow up?"

"They marry."

"Then what do they do?"

"What their husbands tell them to: spin and weave, cook and clean. Take care of their children."

"Then I will stay a maiden," Atalanta said. "I'll roam through the woods, and hunt and shoot, like you."

I approved, but warned her, "Aphrodite gets offended when girls want to stay free. Therefore, don't neglect her altars. You'd do well to bring her gifts of barley cakes and fruits and such."

It was good advice. I should have heeded it myself . . .

Around that time, in nearby Calydon, *my* altars were neglected. It seemed the Calydonians had forgotten me. I thought, I'll send them a reminder . . . I sent them a ferocious boar, twenty feet tall, with tusks as long as an elephant's and spear-sharp bristles jutting from his neck.

Heroes came from near and far to help the Calydonians hunt down this savage beast.

"*I* want to join the hunt," Atalanta said.

I encouraged her, "You're ready. Show the world what you can do."

Off she went, high spirited, well armed, well trained.

If it had been some other girl, the hunters and heroes would have jeered, made cruel fun. But Atalanta's confidence impressed them. So did her beauty. And they welcomed her.

The gigantic boar came charging, speedy on his trotters, evading spears and arrows, impaling hero upon hero on his tusks.

Finally an arrow struck him under the left ear. Blood spurted out and stained his bristles red. It was a Calydonian spearsman who then hurled the spear that pierced the monster's throat and pinned him to the ground. But it was Atalanta's arrow that had slowed him down.

Word spread far and wide about the girl who was as keen a hunter as a man.

King Iasus of Arcadia heard about her, and asked that she be brought to him.

Atalanta came.

"Welcome!" Iasus took her hand, and saw the heart-shaped birthmark on her wrist. "My long-lost child! I thought that you were dead! Oh joy! I'll choose you a rich king to marry, and you'll give me a grandson for an heir. Oh happiness, at last!"

"I don't want to marry," Atalanta said.

"Nonsense. You can't refuse."

"I do refuse," said Atalanta.

Iasus said, "Because it's you, and I'm so glad to have you back, I'll go against the custom of our land. I'll allow you to choose your own husband."

"Good," said Atalanta. "Let's hold races. I'll marry whoever outruns me." She was sure that no one could. "And let the losers all be killed." She thought this would discourage many suitors from entering the race.

But many came, and ran, and lost, and died.

The last suitor to appear was a very fast runner called Melanion. He fell in love with Atalanta the first moment that he saw her, and he desired her so keenly, that it made him even faster.

At the first curve of the track, Melanion spurted ahead. For once Atalanta lagged behind. She doubled her pace. But just as she was about to catch up, he threw down something shiny, round. It rolled to her feet—what was it?

A glittering apple, all golden.

She picked it up. This set her back twelve paces. Now she ran even harder. But just as she almost caught up again, he threw another golden apple. She picked it up, and also stole a glance at him. And when she picked up the third golden apple, she glanced at him again. This time he looked back; his eyes met hers. After that, her legs were drained of all their speed.

Who had given him the golden apples?

Who else but Aphrodite? He'd gone to her shrine and asked for her help. And she plucked them for him from the golden apple tree that flourishes in her garden.

Atalanta lost the race. It didn't trouble her at all. And she grew still less troubled when the winner took her in his arms. By then he looked like a young god to her bedazzled eyes.

Melanion was all that mattered to her now. She couldn't wait to marry.

I wished her happiness. But it surprised and saddened me how readily she gave herself to him.

There came a time when even I, despite my firm resolve, fell ignominiously in love. If only I'd taken my own advice and brought offerings to Aphrodite, would she have been appeased and spared me her revenge?

It happened in Crete, my nymph-companions' native island. We had gone there so that they could see their rivers, streams, and mountaintops again. While they were visiting their relatives, I whiled away the morning on a beach, content—or so I thought!—to be alone.

Like children seeing ships and dragons in the clouds, I played at seeing shapes emerge out of the mist that hovered over the sea: a bird, a cow, a camel—

Suddenly a human shape, one altogether real, came into view: Nobly built and giant-tall, he strode from wave to wave. I watched him, and my heart beat fast. A strange excitement took me in thrall.

"Whoever you are, come nearer," I called in a girlish voice I scarcely recognized.

He did, and sat beside me, saying, "I am Orion, the great hunter." He told me fascinating stories: How he'd rid the island Chios of marauding animals. How the ungrateful king, instead of paying a reward, had turned on him and struck him blind. He told how, stumbling eastward through the sea, he came to where the sun shone hottest. There Helios, the sun god, gave him back his sight. "If not for that," Orion said, "I could not now be dazzled by how beautiful you are." He gazed at me with his great, lucent, sea-green eyes. "Now shall I tell you about Eos, goddess of dawn, and how she angered Aphrodite?"

"Yes, tell me."

"Eos was smitten with Ares—god of war, and Aphrodite's favorite lover. She stole into his bed, caressed him with her rosy fingers, then . . ." His voice trailed off.

"Then, what?"

"They made love. Aphrodite caught them and, as punishment, afflicted Eos with insatiable lust. Poor, unhappy dawn goddess, she has to search and search for lovers, ever new ones, and is never satisfied. The better they love her, the sooner she tires of them. Is that not pitiful?"

"Yes, pitiful. Go on."

"Not long ago, she found me sleeping in a forest where I'd hunted—"

"And then?" I asked on baited breath. "Did *you* make love with her?"

"Yes."

"But did you *love* her? Do you still?"

Instead of answering, he pointed to a craggy mountain peak. "Oh Artemis, somewhere up in there lives the king of mountain goats. I want his horns for trophies! I've chased him many times, once or twice I almost caught him, but always he eluded me. Dearest, let us hunt together. You'll bring me luck, I know." He called me Farthest Shooter and Keenest Archer—I've always prized these compliments, but just then "dearest" sounded best to me.

I climbed up to those heights with him. "Look, behind that boulder, quick!" I passed him an arrow. He shot. The king of mountain goats crashed to the ground. And I took greater pleasure in Orion's triumph than if *I'd* shot the beast.

"Take the left horn for a keepsake. I'll keep the right," he said, then spoke about a task a king had asked him to perform. I didn't hear what task, what king; I heard only the words he did not speak: "I'm leaving."

I asked him to come back, and soon. He said he would.

A year, or ten, or centuries can pass, and we goddesses perceive it as not much longer than a day. But Orion's absence left me so unlike myself, so *wanting*, that even one day's waiting was too long.

Four dawns, four dusks went by. On the fifth morning, Apollo came to Crete. He ran to me, held out his arms.

We're always glad to see each other after absences. But I stayed sitting in the sand.

"Dear sister, you are sad," he said, "I'll cheer you up." He took his lyre, played tunes, and sang me songs.

"You're *still* sad. Come!" He pulled me up, and to the water's edge.

"Look, far far out, almost at the horizon, something's bobbing in the waves."

"Yes, a tiny speck. I see it."

"Artemis, I challenge you to a shooting contest. You shoot first," he said, surprisingly, because he'd always claimed that shooting first was his unquestionable right.

I fetched my bow and arrows.

The tiny bobbing object was the farthest target I had

ever aimed at. Even so, my arrow met its mark. It bobbed one final time and then grew still.

"Winner, I salute you." Apollo offered me his laurel crown.

But I wanted the target for a trophy.

We plunged into the sea and swam—out to where the water was no longer clear, or blue or green, but thick and red. The red was blood, flowing from the object that had seemed so small and now looked huge. It was Orion, with my arrow through his chest.

I drew it out, hurled it away. I pulled Orion by the shoulders. Apollo pushed him by the feet. We swam to shore with him.

We dragged him onto the beach. I forced his lips to open. I blew my breath into his mouth, in vain.

Apollo shrugged.

I raged, I beat my fists against his chest. "You *knew* it was Orion all along! You tricked me into shooting him!"

"Orion betrayed you," Apollo said. "Where do you suppose he went after leaving you? Back to Eos. They made love, and on Delos, our sacred island! For that alone he deserved to die."

"But by *my* hand? Why did you trick me so?"

I didn't wait for him to answer. I longed to be in motion,

and started running, anywhere, away from my despair.

"I did it for your sake," Apollo called, "to help you win your freedom back!"

I left the beach behind me, ran over dunes, through stubble fields, into a lush forest. It had no paths. No human or immortal feet had ever entered. No shrub, no tree, no sapling was ever felled from there.

I lay down on the soft ground. Sunbeams filtered through the canopy of trees. Afternoon turned into night. The moon arose, and made its journey. When it set, I saw Orion, bow in hand, belt drawn tight, all made of stars, standing in the western corner of the sky.

Those stars, so cool and distant, consoled me not at all.

How is it that some mothers know just when their daughters need them most? My mother came that night, and she consoled me.

Now I awake to sunlit hues of green; to earthy, leafy smells; to songbirds singing. Day has come. I am at home here in the forest, wild and free, at one with my true self.

PART TWO

DEMETER SPEAKS

She's lost, my precious Kore! Who stole my child from me?

Spring has come. The fig, the plum, the cherry trees are bursting into fragrant bloom. The air is mild, abuzz with swarming bees. Up in the oak the cuckoo calls. All around me there's rejoicing. I alone am sorrowful and out of step with merrymaking. I'd rather it were winter, when branches wore their coats of ice, and tender wheat and barley shoots were hidden in the ground.

Plowmen come, as every spring. They offer sacrifices. I turn my back on them, withhold my blessing. Let their oxen stumble, let their plowshares dig no furrows, let no seed be sown. I'd rather that my fields lie fallow. Why should beasts and humans fatten on my crops when I, their goddess, am without my child?

With Kore near, I felt content with who I was: my mother's daughter, and my daughter's mother.

With Kore gone, what's left of me?

My mother, Rhea, rescued me when I was in great need. I'll always be her daughter. But am I still my daughter's mother? Is a mother still a mother if she fails to keep her child from harm?

"Mother, help!" my darling cried in terror. It went through me like a sword blade. It still echoes in my ears.

"Kore! Where are you? What is happening to you?" I could not see her anywhere.

I grow to my highest height. There, now I'm mountain-tall. My eyes are sharper than an eagle's. I scan the landscape all around.

I step onto a jagged cliff, the highest on this island. I peer in all directions, overlooking all of Sicily—and still I cannot see her.

Has she vanished from the earth?

"Zeus, she's *your* child, too!" I shout, and shake my fist up at the sky. "Have you been dethroned? Is someone mightier than you now god-king of the world? Is that why you sat idly by while our daughter disappeared?"

Zeus doesn't answer me.

I tear my queenly headdress from my brow. Let winds blow through my yellow hair! It's beautiful, the poets say.

What good is that to me? I run my fingers through it, disheveling it more. I bring my teeth down on my tongue for having scolded Kore when she let her curls get tangled. Oh, that I could take back all angry words I ever spoke to her!

I shrug my stately mantle from my shoulders. I spread my arms. I wing away, over land and down to where wide-swirling Oceanus flows.

Have pirates captured my poor Kore and sailed away with her? I scan the white-capped waves as far as the horizon, but see no mast or sail.

I screech and squawk (I know the languages of birds) to every passing cormorant and ibis, gull and tern: "Have you seen my daughter?" I describe the tunic she was wearing and her curly reddish hair. They all shake their heads and answer no.

Hermes comes darting through the clouds. He greets me cheerfully, then starts complaining, all in fun: "Alas, I'm just a wretched errand boy! Zeus works me hard; he sends me east, south, west, and north–it never stops!" He sighs and grins. But Hermes is a god of swiftly changing moods. Noticing that I look sad, he turns serious and asks, "What troubles you, Demeter? Confide in me, and maybe I can help."

I tell him about Kore. "Oh Hermes, have you seen her, or heard where she might be?"

He has not. "I'll search for her, I'll ask whomever I chance to meet—" Something distracts him. Excitement flashes in his silver eyes. "Pardon me, Demeter, I have urgent business. I must fly—"

Whoosh, he's off. He has a rendezvous.

A flurry of white wings approaches—it's the doves of Aphrodite. They are harnessed to the chariot made of burnished gold in which she rides to meet her lovers.

Excitement flashes in *her* eyes. She's in a hurry, too.

"Aphrodite, have you seen my daughter?"

"You lost her? My, how careless!" She, the worst of mothers, who, like the cowbird, lets others raise her young, has the insolence to call *me* careless! And off she rushes, to her rendezvous.

I head back toward land.

Three lively girls—no, nymphs!—are playing on the shell-encrusted rocks that jut up from the waves. I choke with grief, because it was to *nymphs* that Kore hurried when she left.

I call to them, "I'm looking for my daughter. Have you seen her?"

One is braiding seaweed into another's hair. The third one shakes her head. "We haven't seen her. We don't know her."

"You must, you surely do. She went off to gather flowers with the river nymphs, your sisters. That was the last I saw of her."

"We're sea nymphs; we don't know the river nymphs. We never saw your daughter. We don't know and we don't care who or where she is," they sing in jeering voices.

Where's the border between grief and rage? In the snapping of my fingers, one, two, three—and, look! Three vapid smiles become grimaces. Three pairs of legs grow scaly, thrash about. And, look again! Those legs are fishes' tails, attached to girlish bodies.

"You *were* sea nymphs; now you're sirens. Stay on these rocks forever. Braid seaweed in your hair, and sing! Entice poor sailors to draw near. Watch them wreck their ships and drown, and you'll be blamed, and feared, and loathed by all."

I turn my back on them, fly on.

I reach the shore. I touch the ground of Sicily that Kore loved. I put my lips to it, and say, "Be known as Kore's Island from now on."

I'm home. How happy we were here! My feet are drawn to our favorite mossy grove with sheltering pine trees all around. Here, on many starlit nights, I sang my child to sleep, and cradled her, and kept her safe.

When does deepest grief become despair?

I climb to my temple on top of the mountain near Enna. I bid my priestesses be silent and clothe me all in black. I take two flaming torches from the altar. I carry them in front of me. For nine days and nights, I wander—through villages and woods and meadows, up hills, down into valleys, along the banks of winding rivers—searching for my daughter without cease.

The tenth day dawns. I lie down in a grassy knoll. I'm weary, drifting into sleep, when Hekate appears.

Mortals fear this goddess. They say she is a sorceress. But she is my good friend. "Demeter, there you are. I've been looking for you. I heard Kore cry out—"

"Where was she? Did you see her?" I ask breathlessly.

"No. But there's one who sees all . . ."

Of course! How could I not have thought of him? Had sorrow dimmed my reason? Or did I wish to spare myself the anguish of recalling Kore's parting promise: to return "before the sun's bright horses reach the summit of the sky"?

Hekate takes my hand. We rise up through the sunlit air.

It's almost noon. Helios's chariot approaches. He is the god whose golden eye sees everything.

He knows what I have come to ask. He names the woods where Kore was. He tells who stole her, how it happened, and by whose consent.

PERSEPHONE SPEAKS

"Kore"—did any goddess ever have a plainer name?

My mother is the great Demeter. She has temples everywhere, and priestesses, and festivals; she is revered in every land where humans till the soil.

One time we were watching her worshipers spread garlands on her altar, and I said, "*I* want to be a splendid goddess, too!"

"So you shall, my darling," Mother said.

Yes, but *when*? I wondered. Next year? Or in a hundred, or five hundred, years? Meantime, I trailed after her like her faithful shadow, and no one noticed me.

Of course I minded, wouldn't you?

We loved each other very much. But she wasn't always pleased with me, and I had my resentments, too.

One day when I was little, we were going to a feast in Zeus's palace. Mother told me who would be there: "Gods and goddesses you know, and some you haven't met before —Eurynome, Eleithia, Mnemosyne—"

"What lovely names," I interrupted, "so melodious and meaningful . . ."

"And yours is *not*?" Her green eyes clouded over. "Don't you like the name I gave you anymore?"

"It's too plain, and just means 'maiden,' 'girl.'"

"What's wrong with that?" She frowned, stooped down, fought with the tangles in my hair (it's reddish, thick, unruly; hers is corn-silk fine and fair), and told me how I should behave: "Greet everyone politely. Smooth your tunic under you before you sit down or recline. Don't talk out of turn. And don't belittle maidenhood. Athena, Hestia, and Artemis are maiden-goddesses, all three, and no less glorious for that."

Yes, but they *chose* it, I thought to myself, and spun out dreamy fantasies all during Zeus's feast of how *I'd* choose to spend eternity.

I had a friend named Cyane. She was a river nymph. One hot summer afternoon, we were playing in a deep, clear pool that her river forms. We splashed, we swam, enjoyed ourselves—till Mother came and scolded, "Kore! Can't you see it's nearly dusk? Don't you know I worry when you're gone so long?" She hurried me away.

Another time great Artemis invited me to hunt with her. Of course I wanted to. But Mother wouldn't let me.

"Why not? Why must I always stay where you can see me?"

"Because I need you near," she said.

"You *need* me? Why?"

"Because you make me young again."

This puzzled me. "But, Mother, you *are* young. We goddesses are always young. You told me so yourself."

"Yes, we are. But always-young is not the same as young-right-now." She sighed, looked wistful. "Young-right-now is —let me see—fresh as morning? Like a bud first starting to unfold? I can't remember anymore. Remind me, Kore, dear."

"It's when you're waiting for something to happen, something astonishing and grand—"

"Yes, and you shiver with excitement—"

"No, with anger," I burst out.

"Anger? Why? With whom?"

"With you. Because you're always watching me."

"And rightly so. That is what mothers do. It's how we keep our daughters safe. Now come with me." She took my hand and led me down the hill.

My mother is the grain goddess. She wakes the seeds that sleep inside the earth and makes them grow. She gives the whole world nourishment, and everyone is grateful for her bounty.

All through my childhood until I was almost grown, I followed her from field to field. I watched her spread her arms out wide, blessing the barley, oats, and wheat, and clover.

Often at sundown we'd visit her temple on the highest of the hills that surround the town of Enna. She'd count the gifts of first fruits and fresh-baked loaves her worshipers had piled up on her altar. How pleased she was! I saw the radiance surrounding her grow brighter. And I wondered, *Do I glow?* I couldn't feel it. If I did, it was from reflected glory.

Long into my girlhood, every night, she tucked me in and sang to me. "I'm too old for cradle songs," I'd say, but she kept on.

One night I started to explain, "Mother, can't you understand? I'm growing up, I have a thirst for–"

She rushed off, came back with honey-sweetened water, a drink to soothe young children when they fret.

"No, it's not that kind of thirst! I'm thirsty to discover what powers I'll have, what kind of goddess I am meant to be. I want my future to begin; I'm parched for come-what-may!"

One morning we were sitting atop a granite rock that humans call "Demeter's throne." It gives a sweeping view of terraced hillsides and of the fertile valley down below.

Mother gazed down on her fields. I looked around for friends of mine, and saw the nymphs Callirhoe, Rhodope, Cyane, and Phaino stepping from their river homes onto the reedy banks. They all carried braided baskets and headed for a flower meadow bordering on poplar woods.

"*I* want to gather flowers, too," I said, already sliding down the smooth side of the rock. But Mother grasped my tunic and held on.

"Mother, let me go, just for a little while."

"Kore, no, I had a premonition. I'm afraid for you."

"What harm can come to me? I'll stay close to my friends; I won't wander off on my own." And I promised, "I'll be back before the sun's bright horses reach the summit of the sky."

Jumping to the ground, I heard the sound of fabric ripping—my tunic. Part of its embroidered border stayed in Mother's hand. I didn't care. I ran and joined my friends.

The meadow was dotted purple, pink, and yellow, with crocuses and irises, hyacinths and lilies.

"We hoped you'd come," Rhodope called.

"We've picked all the flowers," Phaino teased.

Cyane said, "No, we saved you some. Look over there." She pointed to a shady patch of white and purple violets.

The white ones were my favorites. I started picking eagerly; then something in the air drew my attention.

"What is it? Kore, what do you smell?"

"Something wonderful. I can't describe it. Don't you smell it, too?"

"It's just the violets," Cyane said.

"No. It's strange, much sweeter, and it's strong . . ." I felt it taking hold of me.

"Kore, where are you going?"

To the end of the meadow, past trumpet vine, jasmine, honeysuckle thickets—all with their familiar smells. The unknown fragrance pulled me on.

"Come back!" called the nymphs. "Don't go into those woods! Poplars are trees of ill omen—"

Too late, I was there. Or else the woods had come to me. The trees were circling around. Or so it seemed, for I was dizzy, drunk on having breathed too deeply of the scent.

At last I reached its source.

I've always loved flowers. I know each one that grows in Sicily by name. But now I saw a flower I had never seen before. It was star-shaped, many-petaled, and dazzling white, its center rimmed with gold.

How could I have suspected who'd created it, or why?

I knelt, and when I gazed at it from nearer, its dark,

round center seemed to turn into the pupil of an eye—my own, or someone else's—gazing back at me.

It was eerie. I began to tremble.

The ground I knelt on trembled, too. More than trembled: quaked and shook, boomed and thundered, loud as hordes of lions roaring. It cracked and split wide open. A chasm gaped where leaf-strewn forest floor had been.

Some who tell this story say that a luckless swineherd happened by just then and tumbled in, along with all his swine.

Maybe so. I didn't see. I was clinging to a tree trunk, holding on with all my strength, not looking down for fear of falling in.

The roaring subsided. I heard hoofbeats, neighing—or was all this a nightmare from which I'd soon awake?

Four horses, black as night, sprang into view. They pulled a gilded chariot. Its driver leaned forward, arms outstretched—

"Mother, help!" I screamed.

Hands tore me from the tree trunk, swung me through the air and into the chariot.

"You scream in vain," a deep voice said, as dry as bones. "Your mother cannot help you now. You've come too far away from her, too near to my domain."

His tunic and cloak were black. So was his flowing hair. His lips and face were pale. His jet-black eyes—their pupils rimmed with gold!—stared into mine, as though to probe my very soul.

I'd never seen this god before, but knew of him—as who does not? He was the god most feared by all. Oh, I was terrified, but could not look away.

I saw him put a helmet on. Then, suddenly, my eyes stared into blankness. He'd disappeared—but only from my sight. The horses' reins stayed taut as though still in his hand. I still felt his body press against my side, and heard his voice ask, "Now that you don't see me, are you less terrified?"

I answered no—and there he was again!

"It's my helmet," he explained. "I put it on, and can't be seen; I take it off, and reappear. The Cyclopes made it for me. Note how elegantly they embossed it with leaves and serpents intertwining." He slid an arm around my waist, then asked me, "Shall I disappear again?"

"No, don't . . ."

"Don't disappear? Don't hold you? Which?"

I had not breath to answer him. I heard a drumming, loud as hammer blows. I thought it was the horses' hooves, but no—their hooves now trod the air! We'd left the earth behind.

We soared into the blue. Winds tossed the chariot about. It lurched and pitched. The dark god pulled me closer, and I knew what hammered so: my heart inside my breast.

Trying to collect myself, I thought of other maidens when they were taken by a god. What was it like for them?

Europa, for one: When the bull-god rushed into the waves and swam away with her, what else, what more, aside from fear of drowning, did she feel? Did she already know that he was Zeus? And earlier, when she was playing on the beach with her companions, and he'd come sidling over, when he put his head into her lap and offered her his flower crown, was she flustered? Was she flattered? Did she accept it, put it on?

And Leda, what did she feel besides surprise and terror when the giant swan approached and folded her into his snowy wings?

And my own mother long ago, girlish, not yet fully grown, running from Poseidon, and he was gaining on her, in her fear of him was there excitement, too? And just before he caught her, when she changed herself into a mare, was she aware that it would make him want her more? Then, when he had her in his arms, and she could not escape, how did she feel?

"Well? Which shall it be?" the god beside me asked

again. "Shall I not disappear? Or not hold you like this?"

"Don't disappear," I said.

He steered the horses in a curved path through the sky. "I'll take you on a farewell journey. Memorize the mountain peaks. Wave to the clouds. Feast on daylight. Fill your eyes."

I did as he advised. My eyes became like two deep wells. I filled them to the brim with light. My heartbeat slowed. The storm of new emotions the god had roused in me abated and gave way to sheer regret. If goddesses could weep, I would have shed a rain of tears down on the dear, green earth.

"Enough of this realm!" the god exclaimed, impatient now. "I'll show you where *I'm* king!" He lashed the horses, hard. They tossed their heads back, neighing loudly, and plunged straight down. I screamed a second time, this time to my father, "Help your daughter, mighty Zeus!"

"Zeus won't help you," said the god beside me when we were back down on the ground.

"Why not? He can! He has the power!"

"Yes, but I assure you, he won't."

"What makes you so certain?"

"I will tell you: It was Zeus who called the flower into being that you admired so. He named it Narcissus. He gave it the scent you couldn't resist. He made it blossom in the spot where the earth's crust is thinnest. He knew the earth would open there and let me through. His purpose was to draw you to me, so that I could take you by surprise. It was my right. He gave me his consent."

"Your *right*? You have a *right*, because my father gave you his consent?"

"Be calm. You know it is the custom to ask the father of the bride—"

"*'Bride?'* You call me 'bride' and never asked for *my* consent? What do you take me for? A wretched human girl whose father gives her to some crude, ungainly suitor she will loathe?"

"Hush."

We'd come within a foot of the abyss. He brought the horses to a halt and said, "I'll tell you what I took you for: a goddess unsurpassed in loveliness."

I felt the color rising in my cheeks and turned my face away.

"No, look at me. You're even lovelier when you blush." And then he asked me, "Do you know my name?"

I nodded.

"Mortals are afraid to say it. Are you brave? I want to hear it from your lips."

"You are Hades."

"Yes. I'm king of the dead. It came about by drawing lots: Zeus drew Olympus and the earth; Poseidon, the sea; and I, the Underworld. I'm pale and cool, because it's dark and dank down there. But the fluid, *ichor,* that flows like blood through all gods' veins pulsates in mine. I have passions and desires, as do my brother gods. As Zeus has Hera for his wife, so I need, and I deserve, a goddess to be mine.

"But know that I am not like other gods in this: When Eros shoots his darts at *them,* they go from one love to the next. The dart that Eros shot at *me* was fashioned of a rarer gold. The wound it made stays open. The love it woke stays new."

He loosened the reins and shouted, "Home!" The horses spurted forward and down into the chasm. Darkness closed us in.

The drop was dizzying. I gasped and thought, *Is this how mortals feel when they're about to die?*

We landed on a rocky slope. The heart-stopping part of the descent was done.

"We have arrived in my domain," Hades said. "From here on, you're no longer Kore." He touched my forehead with his lips and gave me a new name: "Persephone. But you are trembling. Don't you like it? Isn't it melodious?"

"Oh yes, but dreadful, too . . ."

"Because of what it signifies? Don't be troubled. It's a ceremonial name, befitting Hades' queen. Our subjects won't mistake you for their 'bringer of destruction.'"

The darkness diminished. The terrain we traveled through was marshy, vaporous, and gray. I saw a murky river winding in and out past jagged cliffs.

"That is the River of Woe. It flows into the Wailing River," Hades said. "All rivers in the Underworld flow into the River Styx. We're coming to it now."

Again, the horses left the ground, wafting us above a throng of ghostly figures wrapped in shroudlike river mist, slowly moving–forward, backward–rocking, swaying, merging into one another, making mournful sounds.

"Hades, are those the dead?" I asked.

"Yes."

"Do they want to cross the river?"

"Yes, insofar as ghosts can want."

"And *will* they cross?"

"Some will, some won't."

"Why not?"

"Because their bodies were not buried properly. Or else

because they brought no coin for Charon. Can you see him there beside the mooring?"

"Yes." I saw him in his tattered cloak, pushing ghosts onto the barge, and roughly turning others back.

Those he rejected lifted up their arms to us as we passed overhead.

"Hades, will they ever be allowed to cross?"

"Yes, in a hundred years or so."

"Poor souls! How can they bear to wait so long? How will they pass the time?"

"They'll flitter back and forth along the shore. That's what ghosts do. A hundred years, or two or three, it's all the same to them."

"But I heard them moan. Or were they praying? Did they see me? Do they hope you brought me here to comfort them?"

"Who can say if ghosts have hope?" Hades shrugged. "You mustn't let it trouble you. The Fates, not you or I, decreed their destiny."

The Styx is called "the hated river." As we crossed, I saw, heard, and smelled the reasons why: Its brackish whorls make smacking, sucking noises. It reeks of noxious sulphur and teems with hairy-headed eels and flesh-devouring fish.

Ghostly grooms received us when we landed on the

inner shore. They took away the horses and the chariot. We continued on foot. When we came near to Hades' gates, I heard ferocious snarls and growling. A frightful beast leaped toward us. Six eyes, as large as saucers, blazed from his three ghastly heads. Spittle drooled from his three mouths. He opened them and bared his knife-sharp teeth.

"Down, Cerberus!" Hades kicked him in the side. "Greet your new mistress more politely."

The monster hung his heads and made pathetic growls.

"There, he's sorry." Hades scratched him between all three pairs of ears. "He won't hurt you. He only menaces intruders and keeps the dead from trying to escape. Come, Persephone."

The shadowy figures crowding toward the gates made room for us. As we went through, the deepening gloom assailed me.

I saw three roads ahead. At the juncture where they met, I saw a marble table. On it stood three sets of scales. Behind it sat three bearded men.

"That is the place of judgment," Hades said. "Those are the judges: Minos, Rhadamanthys, and Aeacus. They weigh the deeds the ghostly shades performed in life. Then they direct them to their permanent abodes."

"The road that most must travel leads to the Plain of

Asphodels. That region is as drab and undistinguished as were the lives of those who wander there.

"The second road, least traveled, leads to the pleasant meadows called Elysium, reserved for favorites of the gods.

"The third road leads to deepest Tartarus where gods' enemies are punished. There, Prometheus, who stole fire from Zeus and gave it to mortals, stands helpless, chained to a rock. Every night Zeus sends an eagle to hack through his flesh and feed on his liver. There, also, Sisyphus, who stole and cheated, has to push a boulder up a steep incline, knowing it will roll back down, and he will have to push it up again and again, as long as time endures—"

"Hades, stop, I beg you."

He looked into my eyes. "What is it? Are you ill?"

"It passed. But while you spoke I felt as though Prometheus's chains were biting into *my* flesh. Then I became exhausted, as though *I* were struggling with Sisyphus's boulder. It was the strangest feeling . . ."

"It's called pity," Hades said. "You'd best dismiss it. There's no use for it down here."

He led me into a dense forest. Cedars, oaks, and poplar trees stood tall and close together. Their branches formed a leafy canopy that let no light come through.

And yet I saw a glimmer in the distance.

Was it real? Or did my eyes play tricks on me because I longed for brightness?

Walking on, we came to an amazing sight: an oak, the tallest one, with boughs of brightest gold!

Still more amazing was that Hades, who had snatched me to him with no qualms, now knelt humbly down before that tree and prayed: "Oak, be gracious. Vindicate what I have done." He grasped a shining bough that was as thick around as his strong arm. "If I fail to break this bough from off this tree, then I did wrong to bring you here."

He twisted it, not hard, and it broke free.

"There, you see? What I did was right, it was what the Fates decreed. Persephone, do me the honor, accept this golden bough from me."

I braced myself, I thought it would be heavy, but it was as light as a bouquet of lilies in my arms.

Hades' spacious palace is well furnished. Its many lamps are brightly lit to keep the gloom from seeping in.

In its ceremonial hall stand two jewel-studded thrones. "Yours is the one with emeralds and amethysts," Hades said. "Be seated. How does it feel? Tell me, when you were still Kore, did you ever dream that someday you would be a queen?"

"No."

"Well, now you are, and of a realm more vast, more populous than any realm on earth. Dearest queen, Persephone, can you forgive my taking you against your will?" He reached across the narrow space between our thrones. He pressed my hand, and I could feel how much he wanted me to answer yes. I nearly did. But just then my mother's anguish that she'd lost me burst into my mind. And I stayed silent, gave him no reply.

As a husband, Hades proved attentive and respectful, generous, too. (He's rich; he owns all treasures hidden in the earth.) He gave me many gifts; arranged distractions; provided company, permitting Hermes and, on occasion, mortal heroes, not yet dead, to visit our realm.

Also—and this is most unusual in a god—Hades proved faithful—well, almost. He did betray me, once.

He brought a nymph called Mintha to our palace—to be a lively friend for me, I thought.

But then I caught the two of them embracing. I flew into a temper, knocked her down. I stomped on her. To my surprise (I never knew that I possessed the power to transform!), Mintha shrank beneath my feet. I trampled her from flagrant nymph into a modest little plant with a spicy smell—of mint. The longer I trampled, the more she smelled of it.

I'd also never known that I could harbor so much jealousy.

Hades didn't scold me for punishing his paramour; in fact, it seemed to *please* him—why? Did he take my jealousy for a good omen? Did he believe—this gave me pause—that I'd begun to love him?

On many nights (which are no different from days down here, except that we extinguish all the lamps), I lay awake beside him, wondering: Was it true? Had I begun to, *could* I love him? If not, or if not yet, what emotions *did* I feel?

His kindnesses, though many, had not erased my memory of our first encounter. Its mix of thrill and terror, though, had changed, had turned into—what should I call it?—fondness? Yes, I cared for him. And his caresses pleased me.

On other nights, I couldn't sleep for missing Mother and the earth. And on still other nights, for thinking of the subjects in Hades' realm and mine—poor, wretched ghostly shades!

Every day, I saw them drifting idly, aimlessly about, empty-eyed, bereft of memories and expectations, imprisoned in their dismal half-existence without end. And everywhere I went, they reached their arms out, murmuring my name.

Though Hades often said that pity is useless, I could not uproot it from my heart, but neither could I comfort them.

One day, a guest arrived in our realm who *could*.

I walked along the riverbank one morning and saw Charon's rusty barge approaching. As always, it was crowded with the dead. But standing tall among them was a living passenger, as young and handsome as a god–a musician, with an instrument, a lyre, in his hands.

The ghostly shades, and even surly Charon, leaned expectantly toward him.

The river whorls uncurled, grew still when he began to strum the lyre. Gulls and vultures hovering above the barge ceased screeching. The straggly trees along the bank bent forward, as though they'd suddenly grown ears with which to listen.

The barge arrived. The ghostly shadows disembarked. The godlike passenger strummed on. Cerberus came trotting peaceably and listened.

Then Hades strode toward the dock, commanding, "Lyre-strummer, stop! Who are you?"

"I am Orpheus. My father is the king of Thrace. My mother is the Muse Calliope."

"What business brings you here?"

"My loss." He turned these simple words into a dirge

of sorrow. And everyone who heard was moved.

Then he began his story:

"I lost my newly wedded wife, my sweet Eurydice, too soon! She ran headlong through a meadow, fleeing from a cruel man who wanted to dishonor her. She stepped on a poisonous serpent. It bit her in the foot and she died.

"All mortals must come here when our life span ends. But my beloved wife was in the first bloom of her youth—too young! I know you will not *give* her back. But Hades, I beseech you, *lend* me my Eurydice, if only for a while!

"This lyre can't make music without fingers strumming it. Nor can I live without my love. Oh, let me take her home with me. And I'll thank you as long as I live."

"Let him, let him," echoed all the ghostly shades.

The three judges (they had come to listen, too) spoke as one: "Yes, lend him his Eurydice."

"I cannot." Hades shook his head. "Or I would break the law by which I rule: Death must not be undone."

"Then let *me* die," cried Orpheus, and he threw his lyre down.

It lay like a dead thing on the dock. I picked it up. He would not take it from me. But I unclenched his fist. I put the lyre in his hand and folded his reluctant fingers tight around its frame. Then I knelt at Hades' feet and asked, "Release Eurydice."

"I can't. I must not."

"I beg you. Do it for *my* sake."

A silence followed. It seemed endless. A dreadful fear arose in me: What if all music ceased? Then would the whole world turn as sad as our realm down here?

At last Hades gave his answer: "Persephone, to please you, I'll release Eurydice. But I make one condition. Orpheus, take it to heart: You must lead the way. Trust Eurydice to follow. Don't look back, or all your pleading shall have been in vain. Go now. You'll find her on the Plain of Asphodels."

"Wait," I said. "*I'll* make one condition, too."

Hades nodded. "By all means."

"Orpheus, sing to us before you go."

He bowed to me. And then he sang—a song about a mountain: its snows, its groves, its waterfalls, its lynxes, foxes, ibexes, and other wild inhabitants that roam its rugged slopes.

His voice was forceful, tender, bold, and subtle, all at once. When it married with the lyre's tones, the contents of the song—its scene and all its creatures—sprang into the listeners' souls, reviving memories and feelings, yes, even in the pallid, ghostly shades.

It caused such ease in me, I wished that he'd sing on and on.

"Where did you learn your art?" I asked when he was done.

"On Helicon, the Muses' home, the place where I was

born. Calliope, my mother, taught me to sing. The lyre was a present from Apollo, god of music. He taught me how to play."

Then he left us and found his wife amidst the asphodels.

Orpheus led. Eurydice followed. Watching them, I longed for earth more painfully than ever. Oh that I could leave this realm, just once, just long enough to run through fields and meadows in the sweet, bright light of day and gather violets again . . .

The Underworld has neither clocks nor calendars. The weather's always damp and cold. Dawn's rosy fingers never reach us. We don't see Helios drive his chariot across the sky, nor do we see the moon or stars. We're never sure, and hardly care, what day or night or even year it is.

But suddenly I craved to know: What season was it up above? Still spring? How long had I been gone? While Orpheus was singing, I'd felt my mother close to me. And now I felt our absence from each other all the more.

Orpheus failed to win back his Eurydice.

Hermes came and told us how it happened: The long, hard climb was nearly over. Many times along the way, Orpheus had stopped and listened for his dear one's steps. They were so light, they would have been inaudible to any ears but his. The last time he listened, he couldn't hear them anymore. Then he despaired. He turned around—he couldn't help it—and saw her ghostly shadow fade away.

Hermes is the god who guides the dead to our realm. He led her back, returned her to the Plain of Asphodels.

"It's better so," said Hades. "It's right that death not be undone. Persephone, pass me the drinking bowl." He took a gulp of nectar and passed the bowl to Hermes.

Hermes drank and passed it back to me. I raised it to my lips—and set it down. I did not drink. (I knew the law: Whoever eats or drinks down here must stay. Luckily goddesses can fast for long and not lose all our strength.)

"I bring you other news, as well," Hermes said. "Not good news, I'm afraid: There's famine on the earth. The soil has let no seedlings sprout and won't accept new seeds. There are no crops. Mortals are starving. Soon their race will die out—"

"And rush down to me in overwhelming numbers? Hermes, no, that mustn't happen!"

"But it will. And there'll be no one left on earth. No worshipers! No more fragrant smoke from altars, no more sweet wine libations, no offerings of any kind. Zeus is alarmed. He doesn't want to be the god-king of an empty world. Hades, you must help."

"How?" Hades asked.

"It's my mother's help that's needed," I burst out. "Only she can end the famine."

"Yes, but she refuses," Hermes said. "Hades, listen: Demeter wants her daughter back. You had better–"

"No, don't say it! I don't want to hear it!" Hades shouted. "I refuse!"

"You must hear it. Zeus sent me here to tell you, send her back, or the famine will not end."

"I won't. I can't!" Hades brought his fist down on the table. "She is my wife, my queen. She belongs with me! Persephone, say that you do!"

"I belong with Hades–*and* with Demeter, also."

"You can't be in two worlds at once," said my husband. I had never heard him sound so sad.

"Zeus helped you to obtain your bride," said Hermes, calm and firm, "now he commands you: Let her go."

Hades pressed his hands against his head, as though to force his brain to find a way he could hold on to me. Then he asked, "Grant us a moment alone."

Hermes said, "Don't take too long."

Hades led me to his private and secluded garden where shrubs and fruit trees flourish without benefit of sun.

We walked about in silence.

We came to a pomegranate tree. Hades picked a scarlet fruit, pulled off the peel, plucked out one seed, and said, "This seed is little, like the love you feel for me."

"What I feel is not so little."

"Prove it. Do me one kindness. Accept this seed, however small, in place of all the joys I cannot give you. That is all I ask."

He looked so fond and sorrowful, only a goddess made of ice could have refused. I held out my hand.

"No, not there."

He placed the seed between my lips. It was no bigger than a barley grain, and yet momentous, too. I knew I mustn't take it in. But suddenly I felt so hungry . . . After all, I hadn't eaten in so long!

The chariot stood waiting.

Hades kissed me. In my heart I was no longer there.

Hermes drove. The journey took no time at all.

I had prepared myself to see the fields of Sicily all fallow and its meadows dusty dry. But we came another way, emerging in another place, a town called Eleusis. I'll let my mother tell you why.

There she stood!

We ran toward each other. My heart is still too full to tell you more than that she hugged me to her breast.

DEMETER SPEAKS

"**D**emeter, don't be angry," Helios, the sun-god, said, after he'd told me the outrageous story of who'd stolen my daughter, and with whose consent!

"Not angry? Should I be *pleased*? Tell Hades I forgive him? Embrace him as my son-in-law?"

"Be moderate. Consider: He is a god of highest rank, a mighty king, and rich to boot—"

"And savage, violent—he took my child by force!"

"But remember, Zeus allowed it."

"Should I give *thanks* for that?"

"He rules us all." Helios lashed the horses; they sprang into motion. "He wills the day to hurry on, and so must I. Resign yourself. We all must bow to Zeus."

"I defy him! No, I will not bow!" I shouted as the chariot speeded on.

Hecate cautioned, "Not so loud, Demeter."

"Why should I be silent? What have I left to lose?" I climbed onto a higher cloud and shouted even louder: "Gods, where is your honor? You speak fine words, you flatter us, then use us any way you please. For shame!

"Hear me, Zeus: You willed our child to Hades. Now it's *my* will against yours! Return her to me from the dead! Until you do, I'll not set foot on Mount Olympus. I'll seek the company of humans—

"Hecate, let go!" She tried to hold me back. I tore away. My anger was like an archer's bow. It shot me from the sky.

I plummeted to Attica, the land where I had come into my power. It was here I first taught humans how to till the soil, sow seeds, and gather in the corn. But that was long ago.

I hid my shining hair under a ragged shawl. I put on dreary garments that old women wear. I summoned warts and wrinkles to my face. I broke a dead branch from a cypress for a cane to lean on, and hobbled toward the city called Eleusis.

The road was long, the weather, warm. And anger dries the throat. I stopped and knocked at a cottage door.

A woman, Misme was her name, brought me a bowl of water. I drained it in a single gulp.

She had a rude son, Ascalabus. He mimicked how I drank, and asked, "Want more, you greedy hag?"

"Mind your manners," Misme scolded. "Go and bring her more to drink."

"In a bucket? In a tub?" Ascalabus laughed so hard that tears ran down his fat, round cheeks.

Suddenly the laughter stopped, and Misme couldn't see him anymore. "Where is my son? He's gone!"

"Not yet, not quite. Look, there—" I pointed to a yellow-spotted lizard darting up the wall.

The lizard turned his tiny head, looked at his mother one last time, and disappeared into a crack.

Poor, dim woman. If she'd realized who I am, would she have begged, *"Undo the change! Give back my son!"*

And would I have obliged?

Perhaps. More likely, not. Anger makes the heart grow hard. Misme stood dumbfounded. I walked out the door.

Outside the city walls, beside a well they call Callichorus, I sat and rested for a while. Three young girls approached and filled their pitchers.

"Poor old granny, you look weary," one girl said. "What's your name?" another asked. "Where are you from?"

The third girl offered, "May we help you home?"

I chose a human name, "I am Dosso. I have no home . . ." I shut my eyes. The craggy mountains of my mother Rhea's island rose into my mind, and I recalled how safe

I'd felt when I was small and she first brought me there.

"Granny, you're dreaming. Tell us, where's your home?"

"It was in Crete. But now I have nowhere to turn." I sighed and told a human story: "Marauding pirates burned down my house. They tied me up; they took me on their ship. It sailed across the broad back of the sea and landed not too far from here. They would have sold me as a slave, had not these aged teeth of mine chewed through the rope that held me bound."

"And you escaped?" They clapped their hands. "Well done! But what will you do now? Where will you go?"

"Find a household where I'm needed. I'm still quite strong, and I can work. I wouldn't ask much pay."

"I know such a household," said the youngest of the girls.

"We do, too." The others nodded.

"Could you be a nurse?" the eldest asked.

"And care for someone ill?"

"No, for a young child."

"Oh yes. I would be glad to hold a baby in my arms again."

"Then come with us."

They led me through the gates of Eleusis, up a steep hill, to a marble palace. "That is our home," they said. "We are the daughters of King Celeus and Queen Metaneira, rulers of this land."

"Come in, sit down." Queen Metaneira showed me to a soft upholstered armchair by the hearth.

"Thank you, no." I chose a lowly stool instead.

A servant woman brought me wine. "Thank you, no, I am in mourning." I asked for barley water with a leaf of mint.

It was brought. I sipped. Its soothing, sweet aroma gave me hope that I'd find consolation here.

"Let me show you my treasure," Metaneira said. She pushed aside a rawhide screen. There stood a cradle. She took the baby out. "This is my little Demophoön. He came as a surprise, a blessing. I'd thought I was too old to bear a child." She brought him to me and laid him in my lap.

A beam of light shone from his eyes to mine. He smiled . . . and so did I, the first time since my grief began.

"You have a way with him," said Metaneira. "Will you be his nurse?"

And I consented, gladly.

Demophoön grew by leaps and bounds into a sweet-natured, fair-featured baby boy. I could not get enough of him, stayed near him day and night.

If he cried in his sleep, I chased his frightening dream away. If he tottered when he tried to stand, I caught him. If he was feverish or hurt, I knew the proper cure. I kept him free of every ill—save one: the shadow that hangs over all mortals.

Each time I imagined this beloved child growing old, I shivered. He would die! Oh, was there nothing I could do?

One chilly night I huddled by the hearth. The fire was burning low—like life in aged mortals.

I quickened it with balsam twigs. Two flames reached up, like dancers, curving, swaying. . . . I indulged in make-believe, as children like to do, and fancied that the flames were human beings—a handsome boy named Ganymede, a lovely girl named Psyche . . .

Why those two?

The answer flashed into my mind: That boy, that girl are young forever—thanks to Zeus. He rendered them immortal. That power and that right belong to Zeus and only Zeus . . . or so he loudly claims.

Those were my thoughts when little Demophoön began to whimper. I rose and crossed the room to where his cradle stood. Bending down, I stroked his soft, smooth cheeks and sang him back to sleep.

A mirror hung above the cradle.

I gazed into that mirror now. I saw past Dosso's folds and wrinkles to my true face. I recognized myself for who I am: The bringer of the seasons. The giver of the grain that feeds all creatures.

What if I withheld that gift of grain? I envisioned the earth with nothing left alive. It made me wonder: *Who's to say I'm not as powerful as Zeus? That I don't have the right to make a human child immortal?* I shuddered, and resolved, *Well, then, I'll try.*

But how?

The fire on the hearth had burned itself out. None-theless, a golden flame leaped up. I saw it in the mirror, and suddenly I knew what I would do.

I stoked the embers. They still glowed. I brought kindling, twigs, and branches. They ignited. "Fire, do my bidding!" I commanded, and blew my deathless breath on it.

At midnight, in the silence, I picked up Demophoön and laid him down amidst the flames. He smiled sweetly up at me, was not the least afraid.

For three nights I placed him in the flames. And every morning when he woke, back in his cradle, the radiance surrounding him shone brighter.

But on the fourth night, Metaneira smelled the smoke, ran down the stairs, and saw, and shrieked, "You've killed my Demophoön!"

"Not so." I took him up and held him. "He's safe, unharmed. This is a cleansing fire. It burns away mortality."

"Then will he live forever?"

"One more night, and yes, he would have."

She threw herself before the fire, blew her mortal breath on it, and shouted, "Put him back!"

"Too late."

"You won't? I *will*!" She reached for him.

"No, don't. The fire would burn him. It's like other fires now."

"Evil witch, give back my child!" She snatched him, howling, from my arms. She thrust him in his cradle and came at me with her fists—then stopped and stared with bulging eyes as I grew to a tremendous, ceiling-tall height.

I took off my ragged shawl. My shining hair cascaded down. I shed my dreary garment and stood before her as I am.

My radiance flashed through the palace. King Celeus, the princesses, and the servants woke, rushed from their chambers, and were daunted. They fell to their knees.

I turned my back on them—on humans all.

I'd entered this palace in human form. I left it as Demeter, splendid, but with empty arms, my purpose brought to nought, and rage inside my heart.

I strode down the hill, out through the city gates, and to

the well Callichorus. "Be dry as bone," I said, and all its water disappeared.

I strode into the plain that I'd made fruitful long ago, and cried, "Green fields, why do you thrive when I am severed from my child?" I stripped the fronds from off the stalks, ripped open the husks in which the tender ears of corn were ripening, and threw them down. I wrenched the stalks out by the roots.

I trampled on the ground. I flattened the furrows that farmers' ploughs had dug. I waved my arms and shouted, "Crows and starlings, greedy blackbirds, come! Devour all the seeds!"

I climbed to my temple on the hill above the desiccated well, and stood with arms outstretched, as when I used to bless the crops. But now I cursed the land: "Bring nothing forth. Let hunger rule the world."

I put an end to summer. I let the seasons run amok. I froze the earth with ice and snow, then brought on torrid heat, then floods, then drought, then frost again, in dizzying succession.

Zeus said, "This must cease," and sent down his messengers.

The first to come was Iris. She tried to please me, putting rainbows in the sky, and urged, "Be reasonable, restore the order of the seasons! Come back to Mount Olympus!"

"I will," I answered.

"When?"

"When Zeus convinces Hades to release my child. When I have her back, and not a moment sooner."

The next messenger, Hephaestus, tried to bribe me with a necklace. "Look, I made it myself. It's of the rarest, richest gold, and you can have it if you'll take back your curse and let the earth bear fruit."

"Not until my child returns."

Then came Apollo, Athena, the Titaness Metis, the sea-goddess Thetis, and many more, and all in vain.

I let the earth grow iron-hard. And everywhere more people, oxen, sheep, and bulls and heifers starved.

I sat alone beside my temple, deserted as all temples were, and cried to Zeus, "Now do you miss the smoke that wafted up when worshipers burned offerings on our altars? What pleasure will you have from ruling the whole world when not a single mortal is left alive?"

Zeus took these words of mine to heart and sent Hermes down to the Underworld. Hermes persuaded my daughter's captor to do what Zeus commanded. At once. Without delay. You already know this part of the story. You heard it from my daughter's lips.

Of course I didn't know this. I'd given up. I believed she

was forever lost to me. So, when the dreadful noise began, I thought it was Zeus hurling down a thunderbolt and wished it could demolish me, so deep was my despair.

But the noise came from below: The frozen earth outside the wall of Eleusis cracked and split wide open! Four horses, black as night, sprang out. They pulled a gilded chariot into view. Hermes was the driver. His voice was like a trumpet blare: "I've brought her back!"

Faster than flying, I ran down the hill. In an eye-blink I was there.

"Mother, Mother!"

"My precious daughter."

We were in each other's arms. In one beat my heart grew warm. In one instant all the fields grew green, and every creature near to death revived.

"Demeter, now will you return to Mount Olympus?" Hermes asked, and "yes" was on my lips—

"Mother, wait! There's something you must know."

"What is it, my darling?"

"In all the time I spent among the dead, I took no food or drink. And then"—a quaver came into her voice—"I ate a seed, just one little pomegranate seed."

I heaved a sigh from down so deep, it did not leave me breath to speak the words, "You must return."

She looked away. "I couldn't help it . . ."

I asked, "Did Hades force you to?"

"No. But—but . . ." she blushed. "He was so sad, I couldn't *not*. Oh Mother, can't you understand?"

No. All I understood was that I'd lose her again. I could not bear it! I clutched her by the hand and ran. I pulled her up the hill into my temple.

I locked the doors. I pushed two heavy altars up against them—as though such makeshift measures could stave off what had to be.

Night fell. The candles burned down. And yet the temple was aglow with a luster that exceeded the radiance around Persephone and me. The messenger—the very last one Zeus sent down—had come.

It was my mother, Rhea.

She held me with her right arm, my daughter with her left. Linked together, with Rhea in the middle, we were like a three-leaved clover. Her closeness gave my motherhood new strength. My daughter's closeness caused me to remember how it feels to be as young as she. I looked into her eyes and saw what I'd been blind to. Now, yes, I understood, because I *felt* it in *my* heart, what had moved Persephone to eat the seed.

Rhea sat down on the temple steps. "You two look

pale and thin," she said. "Come, rest yourselves, see what I brought you."

We lay down, I to her left, my daughter to her right. We put our heads in her soft lap.

She fed us tasty mouthfuls of ambrosia. "Zeus misses you. He wishes you'd come back and take your rightful place on Mount Olympus," she said to me. To Persephone she said, "You will go back to Hades." And now I could bear it because I saw my daughter's subtle smile, and knew she wanted to.

"For half the year," my mother said. "The other half you'll spend with your dear mother. Is this agreeable to you both?"

It was, it is.

I am at peace.

The earth bears fruit. The seasons follow, one after the other, summer, autumn, winter, spring.

When autumn comes, Persephone goes down among the dead, there to resume her role as Hades' wife and queen. And every year, as surely as the spring returns, so does my beloved daughter. And every time that we embrace, our pleasure in each other is renewed.

NAMES AND PLACES

Actaeon (ak-TAY-on)—A young hunter.

Aeacus (ah-ee—YA-kus)—A son of Zeus and a river nymph, he is one of three judges of the dead.

Aphrodite (af-ro-DY-tee) {Roman Venus}—Born of sea foam, she is the goddess of beauty and love.

Apollo (ap-POL-o)—Also known as Phoebus Apollo, son of Zeus and Leto, twin brother of Artemis, he is the god of prophecy and of the arts, especially music.

Arcadia (ar-KAY-dee-ya)—The central region of the Peloponnese (the wide peninsula of southern Greece). Poets describe it as an idyllic, peaceful land of shepherds tending flocks and as the home of the goat-god Pan.

Ares (AH-rayz) {Roman Mars}—A son of Zeus and Hera, he is the god of war.

Artemis (AR-tay-miss) {Roman Diana}—Daughter of Zeus and Leto, twin sister of Apollo, she is the goddess of hunting and the wilderness.

Ascalabus (as-ka-LAH-bus)—Misme's son, a rude boy who laughed at Demeter.

Asteria (ast-TEER-ee-ah)—A daughter of Coeus and Phoebe, sister of Leto.

Atalanta (at-a-LAN-tah)—A girl raised by a she-bear and befriended by Artemis.

Athena (a-THEE-nah), {Roman Minerva}—Daughter of Zeus and Metis, she is the goddess of wisdom, of weaving, and of war.

Attica (AT-tic-ah)—This mainly mountaineous headland in southeast-central Greece contains the fertile plain that is associated with Demeter.

Calliope (ca-LY-o-pee)—A daughter of Zeus and Mnemosyne, she is the Muse of poetry.

Callirhoe (ca-LIR-o-ee)—A nymph-companion of Artemis.

Callisto (ca-LISS-toh)—Favorite nymph-companion of Artemis.

Calydon (CAL-ee-don)—A region in central Greece.

Celeus (SEE-lee-us)—King of Eleusis.

Cerberus (SER-ber-us)—The three-headed watchdog of Hades.

Charon (KER-on)—The ferryman who brings the dead across the river Styx to Hades.

Chios (KEE-oss)—A large Aegean island close to the shore of Asia Minor.

Clio (KLEE-o)—A daughter of Zeus and Mnemosyne, she is the Muse of history.

Coeus (KOY-us)—A Titan, father of Leto and Asteria.

Crete (KREET)—The largest, southernmost island in the Aegean (the sea between Greece and Asia Minor).

Cronos (KRO-nus) {Roman Saturn}—The Titan ruler of the world, he was defeated and replaced by his son Zeus.

Cyclopes (SY-klo-pees)—The three one-eyed giant sons of Gaia and Uranus, god of the sky.

Delos (DEE-loss)—An Aegean island, birthplace of Artemis and Apollo.

Delphi (DEL-fy)—Located in central Greece, at the foot of Mount Parnassus, this was the site of the ancient world's most sacred oracle.

Demeter (de-MEE-ter) {Roman Ceres}—Daughter of Cronos and Rhea, mother of Persephone, goddess of grain, and agriculture.

Demophoön (DAY-mo-fo-on)—Baby son of Celeus and Metaneira.

Dosso (DOSS-o)—The name Demeter goes by, disguised as a servant woman.

Eleithia (el-AY-thee-ah)—A daughter of Zeus and Hera, she is the childbirth goddess.

Eleusis (ee-LOO-sis)—A town in Attica, where the Eleusinian Mysteries, yearly religious rites in honor of Demeter and Persephone, were held.

Enna (EN-nah)—A town in central Sicily.

Eos (EE-us) {Roman Aurora}—Sister of Helios, she is the goddess of dawn.

Eros (AIR-us) {Roman Cupid}—Son of Aphrodite and Ares, he is the boyish god of love.

Europa (ur-O-pah)—A Phoenician princess. Zeus, in the shape of a bull, abducted her and swam away with her to Crete.

Eurydice (u-RI-di-see)—The wife of Orpheus.

Eurynome (u-RI-num-ee)—A river nymph.

Fates—The three goddesses in charge of destiny.

Gaia (GA-yah) {Roman Terra}—The first creature to be born from Chaos, she is the goddess of the earth.

Ganymede (GA-nee-meed)—A handsome prince whom Zeus's eagle brought to Mount Olympus, to serve as cupbearer at Zeus's feasts.

Hades (HAY-deez) {Roman Pluto}—Son of Rhea and Cronos, husband of Persephone, he is the ruler of the Underworld.

Hekate (HEK-a-tee)—A goddess associated with witchcraft and magic.

Helios (HEE-li-us) {Roman Sol}—The sun-god who sees everything.

Hephaestus (hef-EST-us) {Roman Vulcanus}—A son of Zeus and Hera, born lame, he is a builder, metalsmith, and master of many crafts.

Hera (HEE-rah) {Roman Juno}—A daughter of Rhea and Cronos, wife of Zeus, she is the marriage goddess.

Hermes (HER-meez) {Roman Mercurius}—Son of Zeus and Maia, he delivers Zeus's messages, and guides the dead to Hades. He is also god of travelers, thieves, and merchants, and a bringer of good luck.

Hestia (HES-tee-ah) {Roman Vesta}—Daughter of Rhea and Cronos, she is the household goddess, and keeper of the hearth.

Iasus (YA-sus)—King of Arcadia, and father of Atalanta.

Iris (EYE-ris)—A messenger goddess, she also makes rainbows appear in the sky.

Kore (KO-ray)—See Persephone.

Leda (LEE-dah)—A princess with whom Zeus made love in the shape of a swan.

Lelaps (LEE-laps)—A hunting dog Pan gave to Artemis.

Leto (LEE-toh) {Roman Latona}—Daughter of Coeus and Phoebe, sister of Asteria, beloved of Zeus, she is the mother of Artemis and Apollo.

Lipara (Lip-PAH-rah)—An island off the northeast coast of Sicily.

Melanion (me-LAY-nee-on)—He ran a race with Atalanta, won, and married her.

Metaneira (met-a-NEE-rah)—Queen of Eleusis, wife of Celeus, mother of Demophöon.

Metis (MAY-tiss)—Goddess of mindfulness, beloved of Zeus, and mother of Athena.

Minos (MY-nus)—Son of Zeus and Europa, King of Crete, and one of three judges over the dead.

Mintha (MIN-tha)—A nymph seduced by Hades and punished by Persephone.

Misme (MIZ-mee)—She was the mother of Ascalabus.

Mnemosyne (mnem-O-si-nee)—Goddess of memory, she is the mother, by Zeus, of the nine Muses.

Morpheus (MOR-fee-us)—Son of Hypnos, god of sleep, he is the god of dreams.

Mount Cithaeron (kit-EYE-ron)—A mountain in southeastern Greece.

Mount Leucus (LOO-kuss)—A mountain in Crete.

Mount Olympus (o-LIMP-us)—The highest peak in all of Greece.

Mount Parnassus (par-NASS-us)—A high mountain in southern Greece, sacred to Apollo and the Muses.

Muses (MEW-zes)—Nine daughters of Zeus and Mnemosyne, they are the goddesses of the arts.

Niobe (NI-o-bee)—A proud queen who boasted that having twelve children made her superior to Leto, who only has two.

Olympians are the twelve major deities—Aphrodite, Apollo, Ares, Artemis, Athena, Demeter, Dionysus, Hera, Hermes, Hestia, Hephaestus, and Zeus—who dwell in palaces on top of Mount Olympus.

Orion (o-RY-on)—A giant hunter, loved by Artemis.

Orpheus (OR-fee-us)—The great musician who tried to bring his wife back from the dead.

Pan—A son of Hermes, he is god of pastures, goats, and sheep.

Persephone (per-SEF-o-nee) {Roman Proserpina}–Daughter of Demeter and Zeus, wife of Hades, queen of the Underworld.

Phaino (FY-no)–A river nymph.

Phoebe (FEE-bee)–A Titaness, she is a goddess of the moon, and mother of Leto and Asteria.

Phoebus (FEE-bus)–See Apollo.

Plain of Asphodels (ASS-fo-dels)–A region in the Underworld where pallid flowers bloom.

Poseidon (po-SY-don) {Roman Neptunus}–A son of Cronos and Rhea, he is god of the seas.

Prometheus (pro-MEE-thee-us)–A Titan, enemy of Zeus, he stole Zeus's fire, and gave it to humans.

Pytho (PY-tho)–Part serpent, part hag, she guarded the oracle of Delphi.

Rhadamanthys (rah-dah-MAHN-this)–A son of Zeus and Europa, he is one of the three judges of the dead.

Rhea (REE-ah)–A Titaness, daughter of Gaia and Uranus, wife of Cronos, mother of Demeter, Hera, Hestia, Poseidon, Hades and Zeus.

Rhodope (ro-DOH-pay)–A river nymph.

Sicily–An ancient Greek colony south of mainland Italy, this was Persephone's favorite island.

Sisyphus (SIS-ee-fuss)—He had to push a boulder up a slope in Tartarus forever. This was his punishment for having lied and been a trickster while alive.

Styx (STICKS)—One of the rivers of the Underworld.

Tartarus (TAR-tar-us)—The deepest, darkest region of the Underworld.

Thebes (THEEBZ)—A major city in central Greece.

Thrace (THRAYSS)—A non-Greek land on the northern shore of the Aegean Sea.

Titans and **Titanesses**—Sons, daughters, and grandchildren of Gaia and Uranus, they were gigantic deities preceding the Olympians.

Typhaon (TY-fa-on)—Monster son begotten by Hera on her own, he was the relentless pursuer of Leto.

Underworld, also known as Hades (HAY-deez)—The mythical realm of the dead down underneath the Earth.

Uranus (u-RAY-nus)—Gaia's mate, whom she begot out of herself, is god of the sky.

Zeus (Zoos) {Roman Jupiter}—Youngest son of Rhea and Cronos, he defeated his father and became new ruler of the world.

SOURCES

ANCIENT:

Aeschylus. *Prometheus Bound. Greek Tragedies,* Volume I. Edited by David Grene and Richmond Lattimore. Chicago, IL: The University of Chicago Press, 1942.

Apollodorus. *The Library, Epitome* – Greek myth retellings from the second century B.C. Translated by Sir J.G. Frazer. Cambridge, MA: Loeb Classical Library, Harvard University Press, 1921.

Callimachus. *Hymns and Epigrams* – Greek poems from the third century B.C. Translated by A. W. Mair and G. R. Mair. Cambridge, MA: Loeb Classical Library, Harvard University Press, 1921.

Hesiod. *The Homeric Hymns, and Homerica* – writings from the eight century B.C. that tell how the world began and about the generations of gods and goddesses. Translated by H.G. Evelyn White. Cambridge, MA: Loeb Classical Library, Harvard University Press, 1914.

The Homeric Hymns & The Battle of the Frogs and the Mice. translated by Daryl Hine. New York, NY: Atheneum, 1972.

Homer. *The Iliad* – Epic poem from the eighth century B.C. about the Trojan War. Translated by Richard Lattimore. Chicago, IL: The University of Chicago Press, 1951.

———. *The Odyssey* – Epic poem from the eighth century B.C. about Odysseus's long, adventurous voyage home to Ithaca from Troy. Translated by Robert Fagles. New York, NY: Viking, 1996.

Ovid. *Metamorphoses* – Greek myths with emphasis on transformation, retold by a Roman poet of the first century B.C. Translated by Rolfe Humphries. Bloomington, IN: Indiana University Press, 1955.

Virgil. *The Aenead* – The story of how the Trojan hero Aeneas founded Rome, told by a Roman poet of the first century B.C. Translated by Robert Fitzgerald. New York, NY: Random House, 1981

OTHER:

Bell, Robert E. *Women of Classical Mythology: A Biographical Dictionary*. New York, NY: Oxford University Press, 1991.

Benson, Sally. *Stories of the Gods and Heroes*. Illustrated by Steele Savage. New York, NY: The Dial Press, Inc, 1940

Bowra, C.M. *The Greek Experience*. Cleveland, OH: The World Publishing Company, 1957.

Bulfinch, Thomas. *Myths of Greece and Rome*. Compiled by Bryan Holme. New York, NY: Penguin, 1979.

Finley, M.I. *Aspects of Antiquity: Discoveries and Controversies*. New York, NY: Penguin, 1960.

Grant, Michael, and John Hazel. *Who's Who in Classical Mythology*. London, England: J.M. Dent, 1993.

Graves, Robert. *The Greek Myths*. New York, NY: Penguin, 1955.

Hamilton, Edith. *Mythology*. Boston, MA: Little, Brown, 1942.

Kerenyi, Carl. *Eleusis: Archetypal Image of Mother and Daughter*. Bollingen Series LXV.4, Princeton, NJ: Princeton University Press, 1967.

Kirk, G.S. *The Nature of Greek Myths*. New York, NY: Penguin, 1974.

Rose, H.J. *A Handbook of Greek Mythology*. New York, NY: E.P. Dutton, 1959.

Sacks, David A. *Dictionary of the Ancient Greek World*. New York, NY: Oxford University Press, 1995.

Seyfert, Oskar. *Dictionary of Classical Antiquities*. Cleveland, OH: Meridian Books, 1956.

Vernan, Jean-Pierere. *The Origins of Greek Thought*. Ithaca, NY: Cornell University Press, 1982.

———. *Mortals and Immortals*, Princeton, NJ: Princeton University Press, 1991.

———. *The Universe, the Gods, and Men: Ancient Greek Myths*, translated from the French by Linda Asher. New York, NY: Harper/Collins, 1999.